MALLORY
KANE

THE SHARPSHOOTER'S SECRET SON

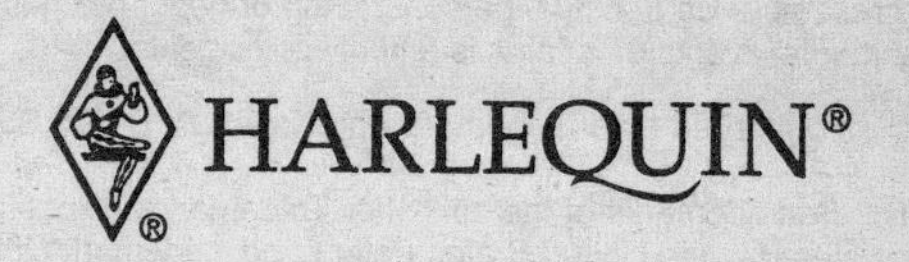

TORONTO • NEW YORK • LONDON
AMSTERDAM • PARIS • SYDNEY • HAMBURG
STOCKHOLM • ATHENS • TOKYO • MILAN • MADRID
PRAGUE • WARSAW • BUDAPEST • AUCKLAND

For Debbie and Lorraine

ISBN-13: 978-0-373-69429-7

THE SHARPSHOOTER'S SECRET SON

This edition published by arrangement with Harlequin Books S.A.

www.eHarlequin.com

Printed in U.S.A.

He had one chance to prove himself worthy of being a father.

She hadn't seen him in eight long months, although she'd come close to telling him about the baby. Then she'd thought better of it, decided that she and her child would be better off if she never got sucked into his self-destructive life.

Seeing him now, she wasn't sure she'd made the right decision.

Loving Deke was a recipe for disaster. Not that her heart cared. Nor her body. He'd always been the sexiest thing on the planet. From his sun-streaked brown hair to his startling sea-blue eyes. From the hard line of his jaw to his broad, leanly muscled shoulders. Even his battered shearling jacket couldn't hide the power and grace of his six-foot-plus body.

She squeezed the hand that held hers and knew she had no other choice but to give in with a whispered "Take me."

ABOUT THE AUTHOR

Mallory Kane credits her love of books to her mother, a librarian, who taught her that books are a precious resource and should be treated with loving respect. Her father and grandfather were steeped in the Southern tradition of oral history, and could hold an audience spellbound for hours with their storytelling skills. Mallory aspires to be as good a storyteller as her father.

Mallory lives in Mississippi with her computer-genius husband, their two fascinating cats and, at current count, seven computers. She loves to hear from readers. You can write her at mallory@mallorykane.com or via Harlequin Books.

Books by Mallory Kane

HARLEQUIN INTRIGUE

620—THE LAWMAN WHO LOVED HER
698—HEIR TO SECRET MEMORIES
738—BODYGUARD/HUSBAND*
789—BULLETPROOF BILLIONAIRE
809—A PROTECTED WITNESS*
863—SEEKING ASYLUM*
899—LULLABIES AND LIES*
927—COVERT MAKEOVER
965—SIX-GUN INVESTIGATION
1021—A FATHER'S SACRIFICE
1037—SILENT GUARDIAN
1069—THE HEART OF BRODY McQUADE
1086—SOLVING THE MYSTERIOUS STRANGER
1103—HIGH SCHOOL REUNION
1158—HIS BEST FRIEND'S BABY†
1162—THE SHARPSHOOTER'S SECRET SON†

*Ultimate Agents
†Black Hills Brotherhood

CAST OF CHARACTERS

Deke Cunningham—The air force made a man out of him and taught him responsibility and honor. Then a promise he made placed him in an impossible situation. A secret of international importance rests on his shoulders, but a much worse burden weighs down his heart.

Mindy Cunningham—She has always been in love with bad-boy Deke Cunningham. But he seemed bent on destroying himself and her. Now she's pregnant with Deke's baby and entangled in his life again. Can she trust this man who has broken every promise he ever made her?

Frank James—The alias of the terrorist who has kidnapped Deke's ex-wife to get to him. He knows too much to be working alone, but who is his mole inside BHSAR?

Irina Castle—Her belief that her husband is still alive has almost bankrupted Black Hills Search and Rescue and nearly cost the life of one of her specialists. Now her obsession has put another of her husband's friends in danger.

Aaron Gold—His computer expertise is invaluable to BHSAR. But is he the grateful son of an American hero who died on a mission under Rook Castle's command, or a bitter young man who blames Rook for his dad's death?

Brock O'Neill—This former navy SEAL can get the job done, but nobody knows much about him. He's terse and secretive about his private life, and no one knows where he came from or where he goes when he disappears.

Rafiq Jackson—Rafiq was born in England of an Iranian mother and a British father. He speaks several languages and is a mathematical genius who worked for the NSA. But where does his loyalty lie?

Chapter One

They called them ghost towns for a reason.

Black Hills Search and Rescue Specialist Deke Cunningham wasn't afraid of anything. Not anymore. But the late afternoon shadows spooked him. They moved with him, reaching out like gnarled fingers across the empty, dusty main street of Cleancutt, Wyoming. He tried to shake off the feeling, but it wouldn't shake. Probably because today he wasn't working a routine assignment to rescue a deserving but nameless innocent.

Today he was searching for his ex-wife.

He glanced at the GPS locator built into his phone, then at the two-story building with the letters *H E L* barely readable above the door. The *O* and the *T* had long since faded.

This was it. The location where BHSAR computer expert Aaron Gold had finally managed to triangulate Mindy's last cell phone transmission.

Mindy. She didn't deserve this. She hadn't deserved anything she'd gotten for loving him.

And he'd never deserved her.

Deke approached the two-story building, doing his damnedest not to swipe his palm across the nape of his neck, where prickles of awareness tingled. He was being watched.

No surprise there.

He even knew who was watching him. The same person who'd kidnapped his ex-wife. Well—who'd *ordered* her kidnapped, anyhow.

Novus Ordo. The infamous international terrorist who'd already targeted another member of the BHSAR team, Matt Parker.

We've got your wife, the obviously disguised voice on the cell phone had said.

Alarm bells had clanged in his head and his gut had clenched with worry. Still, he'd had to smile a little. Whoever the kidnapper was, he had no idea what he'd gotten hold of when he'd grabbed Mindy Cunningham.

"Ex-wife," he'd muttered, working to sound bored and uninterested. "And be my guest. You can have her."

"This is no joke, Cunningham. We've got her and we'll kill her if you don't do what we say."

"The only thing I think you've got is her cell phone and a death wish."

The kidnapper had taken the bait. He'd put Mindy on the phone.

Deke Cunningham, don't pay them one red cent! It's a trap—

Tough words. Exactly what he'd expected from her. But beneath her brave words he heard fear—a soul-deep terror he'd never heard in her voice before. And that, more than anything the kidnapper said, scared him to death.

Something was wrong with her. Something beyond being kidnapped. While that alone would be enough to terrify any woman, his Mindy was made of stronger stuff.

In the twenty years since he'd first spotted her hanging by her heels from the top rung of the elementary school jungle gym, he'd never seen anything she couldn't handle.

Except him.

Her tight, strained voice, cut by static, still echoed in his head as he paused at the bottom of the dilapidated wooden steps of the only hotel in Cleancutt, Wyoming.

He'd heard about the ghost towns of Wyoming all his life. Eighty years ago, Cleancutt and other coal-mining camps had been booming towns. But by the 1950s, underground coal mining had given way to strip-mining, so today Cleancutt was a ghost, a dying piece of history located near the city of Casper.

A vibration started in his breast pocket. *Damn it.* His phone.

As he retrieved it, he glanced around him, in case he could catch someone watching him, waiting for him to answer. But the display read Irina Castle, his boss, not Mindy. He pressed the talk button without saying anything.

"Deke, where are you?" Irina asked.

"I'm busy," he said quietly.

"You did it, didn't you? You went after Mindy alone. I told you to wait until I could arrange a meeting with Aaron Schiff."

"Irina, do *not* get the FBI involved in this. It's too dangerous for Mindy. I'll handle it. Besides, you know the drill. They threatened to hurt her if I brought backup."

"And *you* know the drill. My specialists never take unnecessary risks."

"This one was necessary."

Irina blew out a sigh of frustration. "You told Aaron not to tell me where you are." Her voice was accusatory.

"It's for your own good, and Mindy's. You can't know. It's too dangerous for you. Besides, there's nobody alive who's better trained to run a covert rescue mission than me." He'd meant the comment to be reassuring, but it hung in the sudden silence between them.

Irina's husband, Rook Castle, had been the best until he'd been assassinated by Novus Ordo two years ago.

"Aaron and Rafe have my projected timeline," he continued. "They know what to do. You've got to trust me, Irina."

"I don't like it."

"You think I do? I should have known what was going to happen as soon as Matt told me he'd been followed back here from Mahjidastan. I should have anticipated that Novus would go after Mindy."

Novus Ordo was desperate to find out why Irina had suddenly called Matt Parker back from assignment in Mahjidastan and announced to her employees that she was ending her two-year-long search for her husband—or his body.

"It's not your fault, Deke."

"The hell it's not. I should have taken care of her, put her in protective custody." He shook off the feeling of failure. He'd let Mindy get captured. Now he had to rescue her.

"Don't worry, Irina. I know more about Novus than

anyone alive. You listen to Rafe and Aaron and Brock. They each have their instructions. Their primary mission is to keep you safe." He paused. "And Irina, don't leave the ranch without one of them with you. Make sure all three of them know where you're going and who you're going with."

Irina sighed in frustration. "You sound like you don't trust your own team."

"My helicopter was sabotaged. I don't trust anybody but you and me."

"You mentioned your timeline. What is it?"

"I plan to be out of there with Mindy in less than twenty-four hours."

"What's your drop-dead time?"

"Seventy-two." He had his timeline. He wished he knew what Novus's was.

"Be careful, Deke."

He hung up and started to pocket his phone, then hesitated, looking at the display.

Two days ago, the BHSAR recovery team, along with the FBI, had found the body of the man who had tried to get his hands on Matt Parker.

Papers and a prepaid cell phone found on the dead man proved his involvement in terrorist activities, with ties to Novus Ordo. It was bad enough that it took only a couple of hours for Novus to find out that Irina had recalled Matt. What made it so much worse was the ruined helicopter rotor on the floor of Deke's hangar that proved his bird had been sabotaged. The grounded helicopter had caused Deke to miss a critical rendezvous point and had almost cost Matt Parker and Aimee Vick their lives.

There was only one explanation for those security breaches.

Both the sabotage and Novus's intel had to have been engineered by someone who had unrestricted access to Castle Ranch. They had a traitor in BHSAR. Someone who was working for Novus.

Deke had put his most trusted specialists to guarding Irina. He just wished he could trust them without reservation.

But there was only one man in the world, other than himself, whom he could trust with Irina's life.

Trying to ignore the fact that his fingers were shaking, Deke dialed a number he'd thought he'd never call.

Irina's innocent action had negated everything Rook Castle had done to keep her safe.

Deke listened to the electronic message, hoping he was doing the right thing. He spoke quickly, quietly, then hung up.

It was done. Two years ago he'd made a promise to his best friend, Rook Castle. Today he'd broken it. But he'd had no choice. It was time to raise the dead.

DEKE CAREFULLY CLIMBED the crumbling steps and put his shoulder against the weathered front door of the abandoned hotel. He stopped dead in his tracks when it creaked loudly. Clutching his weapon in both hands, he listened.

Nothing. Not a scurrying rat or the buzz of a disturbed insect.

He'd expected Novus to come after him. He'd hoped the terrorist wouldn't be savvy enough to go after his ex-wife. Hell, they'd been divorced over two years.

It disturbed him that Novus knew that much about him. Mindy was his weakness.

His only weakness.

The air force had done what nothing else ever had—it had made a man out of him. He could fly a helicopter. He could shoot a housefly off a general's lapel at two hundred yards—hell, he could take that shot *while* flying a bird.

Being a Special Forces Op had taught him there was nothing he couldn't face and conquer.

But with one disappointed look, and the sparkle of a tear, Mindy could reduce him to his pathetic, arrogant high-school self, trying to bully his way through school and drink his way through life.

He stood outside the hotel's door and wondered what kind of traps Novus had set for him. He'd have preferred a face-to-face confrontation, but he already knew the publicity-shy Novus wouldn't do that.

There was a reason the terrorist wore a surgical mask in every known photo. An excellent reason. And only a few people knew what that reason was.

Yeah, he was walking into a trap. But Novus had baited it with the only lure he couldn't resist.

His ex-wife.

All those thoughts swirled through his mind in the two seconds it took for him to flex his fingers, retighten them around the grip of his Sig Sauer, and take a deep breath.

Here goes.

He nudged the door another inch and slipped through.

The hotel lobby could have been lifted out of one of the Western movies his old man had watched when he wasn't passed out from cheap vodka.

When Deke stepped inside, eyeing the ornate desk and curved staircase, glass crunched under his boot. Shattered prisms from a broken chandelier.

Then something moved at the edge of his vision.

Startled, he swung around. His finger tightened on the trigger.

A raccoon. It scurried across the room, claws clicking on the worn hardwood floor like faraway machine-gun fire.

Deke's breath whooshed out and his trigger finger relaxed. He took another step, eyeing the dark room beyond the arched doorway. He figured it was the dining room.

What was the raccoon running from? He crossed the lobby and angled around the arch so his back stayed to the wall.

Heavy curtains revealed only slivers of the late afternoon sun. The smell of mildew and rotting wood tickled his nostrils. He held his breath, resisting the urge to sneeze as he moved silently across to the shrouded windows and reached up to push the drapes apart. Too late, he saw the flash and heard the report.

Something stung the curve of his cheek. He whirled, ready to shoot, but whirling turned out not to be such a good idea.

Things got real hazy real fast. A fuzzy shadow loomed in front of him. He aimed, but as hard as he tried, he couldn't make his fingers hold on to the gun, and he couldn't make his legs hold him up.

As the room tilted sideways, the haze before his eyes turned to black.

DAMN, HE HATED THE WAITING. He liked to be the one making the phone calls. When he had to wait to be called, he couldn't control who might be listening.

He paced back and forth in front of the big picture

window, with its panoramic view of the Black Hills, until he couldn't stand it any longer. He yanked the blinds shut. He despised those desolate looming mountains. He'd seen enough of them to last him the rest of his life and beyond.

The prepaid cell phone hidden in his shaving kit rang.

Finally.

"Everything's in place here."

"No change here."

"There better be a change soon."

"I'm working on it. Do you have any idea of the level of security around this place? It's tripled since—"

"Do you have any idea of the time constraints we're facing?"

"I think I'm close—"

"You think? You'd better know! We've only got one chance. I'm guessing you remember what'll happen if you fail me."

"Why all the mind games? It'd be a hell of a lot easier to just go in and get it over with."

"Are you questioning my methods? Because you're not indispensable. Nobody is."

SOMETHING SOFT ROCKED against his side, rousing him. His mouth felt stuffed with cotton and his stomach clenched. Beneath the nauseating smell of mildew and rotten wood, he noticed a sweet, familiar scent.

He tried to push through the drowsiness, but whoever had filled his mouth with cotton had put lead weights on his eyelids. He wanted to turn over, but he was too tired.

The unmistakable supple firmness of a female body rocked against him again. "Eee!"

"Mindy, sugar," Deke mumbled. "Move over."

Whoa. A sharp blade of reality sliced through his mental fog. That wasn't right—on so many levels. For one thing, his tongue wasn't working, so all he'd managed to do was grunt unintelligibly.

"Eee, ake uk," she retorted.

What was she saying? Maybe she was dreaming. Maybe *he* was.

"Okay," he whispered, smiling drowsily to himself. "You know what happens when you don't move over." Anticipating her giggles and kisses, he turned—or tried to.

He couldn't move.

He wasn't in bed. He *sure* wasn't in bed with Mindy. That hadn't happened in a long, long time.

So where the hell was he?

More shards of reality ripped through his brain. The flash of gunpowder. The biting sting in his cheek.

He forced his eyes open. It was dark. Totally dark.

Danger! His heart rate skyrocketed and his Special Forces training kicked in.

Judging by the way his head wobbled like a bobblehead doll, he figured he'd been drugged. He clenched his jaw and worked to gather his thoughts.

The gunpowder. The sting. He'd been shot with a tranquilizer gun. Ah, hell.

He bit down on his tongue, using the pain to clear his brain. Giving in to drugs—or fatigue, or torture—in combat rescue missions could be fatal. Not only to the rescuer, but also to the innocents depending on him for their safety, their protection, their very lives.

Before he could help anyone else, he had to assess his own condition. He needed to take inventory.

Blood? No stickiness or wet warmth.

Broken bones? He shifted enough that his arms ached and his legs cramped. No.

Other injuries? Nope. Just the sting from the tranq dart. That and the drug it had delivered.

Location? Somewhere dark and damp.

Position? Tied up—arms behind his back, and gagged. He pushed his dry tongue against the cloth in his mouth. Gagged tight. Then, gingerly, he moved his legs—and nearly fell off the crate.

That explained the cramps. His ankles were tied.

Mission? Not quite as easy. What was he doing here, tied up and drugged?

"Eee!"

Mindy. Her voice ripped the haze from his brain. That was it. He'd come here to rescue her. Novus Ordo had kidnapped her to get to him.

Her soft warmth was close—way too close for comfort. Her shoulder was touching his. Judging by her restricted movements and incoherent mutterings, she was tied up and gagged, too.

He wanted to reassure her, but that would be a waste of breath with the gag in his mouth. So he spent his energy getting rid of it. He rubbed his mouth and chin against his shoulder, not easy with his hands tethered behind his back.

His neck and jaw ached like a sonofabitch, and the skin on his chin was raw by the time the cloth peeled away from his tongue and lips.

His throat was too dry to swallow. "Mindy? You all right?" he croaked.

Her answer was a frustrated growl.

"Okay, okay, just a second." He scooted closer and twisted until he was leaning heavily against her shoulder.

Another not-so-good idea. But this time it was because he got a whiff of that tangerine bath stuff she always used. He bent his head and nuzzled her cheek, feeling for her gag with his mouth.

Soft, warm, tangerine sweetness. That solved the dry-mouth issue. Her familiar scent made his mouth water and his body tighten in immediate, familiar response. He clenched his jaw and swallowed a groan of frustration. Sex had never been the problem between them.

It sure as hell hadn't been the solution.

Mindy stiffened at his frustrated moan, slamming his brain with a harsh reminder that this wasn't old times, it was deadly serious.

But she didn't lash out at him or try to move away. In fact, she angled her head to give him better access to the cloth that gagged her.

He bit and tugged at it with his teeth until it began to loosen. He tried to hold his breath, tried to ignore the soft, sensual tickle of her hair against his nose and cheek.

After a lot of tugging and nibbling and some extremely uncomfortable brushing of his mouth against her lips, cheeks and chin, he finally got her gag loose.

When he straightened, his head felt clearer, although wherever they were was dark as the cargo hold of a C-17 transport plane at midnight. The only light was pitifully dim and came from a window high above their heads.

The smell of mildew and dirt chased away Mindy's familiar, evocative scent.

"Basement," he muttered. They had to be in a basement.

Mindy groaned and wriggled against him.

"Min? Are you okay?" he asked, squinting in the darkness. He could barely make out the silhouette of her face. Her dark clothes blended into a pool of shadows just below her shoulders. "Did they hurt you?"

She shook her head. "Just practically broke my arms when he tied me up." Her normally husky voice was soft and raspy.

And sexy as hell.

Deke cursed to himself. What a chump he was. After all this time, his ex-wife could still turn him on just by talking.

She coughed. "By the way, thanks for involving me in your little adventure."

And she could still tick him off.

He took a deep breath and winced when the blast of air sent a piercing ache through his temples. "Here we go again," he muttered.

"Don't even try to tell me this doesn't involve one of your rescues," she rasped.

"You think I'd put you in danger if I could help it?"

"What I think is that you've gotten yourself in over your head again. You're never going to learn that you can't save everybody. And even if you could, it wouldn't fill up that hole inside you."

Deke grimaced. It was an old argument, and he'd be damned if he let her lead him down that road again.

He raised his gaze to hers and curved his lips in a confident smile, prepared to give her back a smart retort. But even in the dimness he could see the fear that darkened her olive-green eyes. The same fear he'd heard in her voice. It knocked the confidence right out of him.

"Min, are you sure you're okay? You don't sound too good."

She focused on a point somewhere behind him and to his left. Then she arched her neck, and sonofagun if she didn't stick the tip of her pink tongue out to moisten her lips.

Do not go there, he ordered his brain. But it went there anyhow—to all the amazing things Mindy could do with her tongue. Not the least of which was cut him down to size with a well-chosen word.

"I'm—okay," she rasped, then coughed again.

He knew how she felt. Her throat sounded as dry and sore as his. "What the hell happened? How'd they kidnap you?"

"I got a call about some—something addressed to me that had been delivered to the wrong place." Her voice gained a bit of strength as she talked. "When I went to pick it up, they grabbed me."

"Damn it, how many times have I told you—don't go to strange places alone. You know how dangerous it can be."

"Right," she croaked. "Because of your dangerous profession. Well, silly me. Since we've been divorced for two years I was kind of hoping your danger wouldn't rub off on me anymore." Her hand went to her throat.

"Besides, this was a young woman. She told me she was also pr—" She stopped.

"Also what?"

After a split-second pause and a brief shake of her head, she continued: "She said a store had delivered some things to her by mistake. They were addressed to me. She asked if I could pick them up because she was—ill."

"Damn it, Min. That's an obvious scam. I can't believe you fell for it."

"Would you listen to me?" she snapped. "She said the sender's name was Irina."

Deke's scalp prickled. More proof that Novus had deliberately targeted Mindy. He'd expected it, but that didn't mean he liked it.

"The girl said that?"

She nodded. "I should have been suspicious, because Irina wouldn't know— I mean, there's no reason she'd send me a b— a gift out of the blue."

"What's the matter with you? Did they drug you, too? You sound strange."

"As soon as the door opened, somebody dragged me inside and stuck something in my neck. The next thing I knew, I woke up here."

"Did you get a look at them?"

"No. I was blindfolded until they brought you in this morning. He took my blindfold off right before he left. I never saw him."

"But it *was* a man? What did he tell you? Anything? What made you think it had anything to do with me?"

Mindy made a small, impatient noise. He knew the look she was wearing, as well as if she were standing in a spotlight. He'd seen it too many times before. It was her *do not treat me like an idiot* scowl.

"What made me—? Maybe because I've never done anything that would cause anyone to kidnap me. You, on the other hand—"

"Me what?" His evasion was automatic. He'd practiced evading the truth from the time he could talk. It was ingrained in him—part of his survival tactic.

But he knew she was right. He'd done plenty in his lifetime that might make him the target of revenge. Not the least of which had been just two years ago.

A lot of people, including Mindy, would want his head on a pike if they knew what he'd done—for and *to* his best friend. His only friend.

However, what *a lot of people* thought meant nothing. He'd do it again. That and more, for the one man who'd always believed in him—who'd trusted his life to him.

His life *and* his death.

I just hope your sacrifice wasn't in vain, Rook. Because here they were battling Novus Ordo again. And this time he wasn't going to give up.

"Okay, fine," he snapped at Mindy. "Supposing for the moment that I've screwed up your life yet again. I can't change that. But I can do my best to get us out of here. I promise, as soon as I can manage it, I'll get you back to the normal, safe life you like so much."

Chapter Two

If her mouth didn't hurt so much, she'd smile at Deke's words, Mindy thought. *The normal, safe life you like so much.*

She'd give anything for normal and safe right now.

But as usual when Deke was around, normal and safe had left the building.

His words were on target. She'd loved him most of her life, and loving Deke wasn't exactly a recipe for normal. Certainly not for safe.

Loving Deke was a recipe for disaster. Not that her heart cared. Nor her body. He'd always been the sexiest thing on the planet. From his sun-streaked brown hair to his startling sea-blue eyes. From the hard line of his jaw to his broad, leanly muscled shoulders. Even his battered shearling jacket couldn't hide the power and grace of his six-feet-plus body.

A wave of nausea reminded her that this was no time to be ogling her ex-husband. She swallowed against the queasiness that was fast overtaking her. It had plagued her ever since the moment yesterday morning when she'd rapped on the apartment door. Even before the door opened, she knew she'd made a mistake.

Deke had warned her often enough not to wander around strange places by herself. But the message had been so simple, so innocent sounding.

Hi. Mindy Cunningham? I just received a delivery from Babies First that belongs to you. It's from an Irene or Irina Castle. I'd bring it to you, but I'm on bed rest for the last month of my pregnancy. Can you pick it up?

When she got to the address, the person who opened the door wasn't a pregnant woman. Wasn't even a woman. It was a man. Something about him—the expression on his face or the gleam in his eyes—confirmed that she'd screwed up.

Before she could react, he'd grabbed her arm and pulled her inside, slamming the door behind her. Then he'd shoved her up against a wall and stuck something into the back of her neck.

He'd drugged her.

She was terrified that whatever he'd given her might hurt the baby. It was her worst fear—that something might happen to her little Sprout.

As if he knew what she was thinking, Sprout kicked. She rubbed her tummy and smiled sadly.

Until she'd acquired this tiny passenger that depended on her for his very life, she'd have said her worst fear was that she'd never be able to get over the man sitting next to her.

Deke Cunningham, air force veteran, sharpshooter, alcoholic, adventurer and ex-husband.

Once their divorce was final, her plan had been to never see him again. But the best-laid plans…

Just over eight months ago, he'd come to her mother's funeral. One of about three times in his life she'd seen him in a suit. He'd been handsome as a *GQ* model, and more gentle, sweet and protective than he'd ever been before.

For that one night, he was the man she'd always known he could be.

At the end of the evening he was still there, at her house. Just to make sure she was okay, he'd said.

When he got up to leave, somehow she'd asked him to stay. They'd somehow ended up in the bed, and she'd somehow ended up pregnant.

So much for getting over him.

"Mindy, you're not okay. They hurt you, didn't they?"

His voice was controlled—barely, but that was all about him that was. His intensity and anger washed over her like scalding hot water. Anger, not at her, but on her behalf.

"No, I'm not injured. Just tired and hurting."

He'd never understood why she hadn't wanted him to be angry for her. He'd never realized that his anger—even when it wasn't directed at her—still scared her.

And that was why, although he needed to know what he was up against—deserved to—she couldn't tell him. Not until she absolutely had to.

Like the coward she was, she planned to put off that revelation as long as she possibly could, because scalding water didn't begin to describe what Deke would throw at her when he found out she was pregnant—with *his* child.

"Deke, we've got to get out of here. The guy told me he'd be watching me. He'll be back anytime."

"Yeah, we do. Can you move? Turn around. Let me see your hands."

Could she move? Hah. *Not too well,* she wanted to answer. Like an overloaded supply plane, she was carrying heavy on the front end.

She twisted until her back was to him, working to suppress the grunts and groans that went with everything she did these days.

By the time he said "That's good," she was breathing hard.

"Min, are you sure you're okay?"

She squeezed her eyes shut and nodded. "It's the drug," she said as evenly as she could. "It's making me light-headed. And I'm hungry."

He chuckled. "No surprise there."

Mindy bit her lip against the poignant memories that bombarded her. The sweet teasing, the tickling matches, the kisses. Dear heavens, she'd missed him. It didn't matter how many times her head reminded her heart that they were as compatible as jet fuel and an ignition source.

He twisted on the wooden crate until he was facing her back. Then he bent double to look at the ropes binding her hands.

He uttered a short burst of colorful curses. "Damn it, I can't see anything."

"Can you bite them like you did the gag?"

He sniffed in disdain. "My teeth aren't that good. Stay still."

Mindy waited. It soon became obvious that Deke was scooting around until his back was to hers. Then he shifted closer and twisted some more, until they were pressed together like bookends.

She felt his hands on hers, big, warm, protective, as they explored the ropes.

He let go a string of colorful curses. "…Those sons of bitches," he finished.

Mindy's pulse skittered. "What is it Deke? What's wrong?"

"Nobody's this stupid. Everything about this, from the moment you called, has been too easy," he muttered. "Too pat."

"Too easy? How is this easy?"

"They used your phone. Didn't even bother to keep the call short. Like they were telegraphing their location. And now, these knots are just strong enough to be frustrating. If he'd wanted to, he could have used knots I'd never be able to untie."

"That makes sense," she rasped. "I tried to warn you that it was a trap to lure you here."

"Trust me. I'd already figured that out."

Deke's hands moved over hers, touching and manipulating as he worked to loosen the knots.

"Ow!"

"Sorry."

"No, I'm sorry. My thumb got a little twisted."

"I'm almost done."

She listened to his labored breathing as he worked. "Deke, why do they want you? You know who they are, don't you?"

She winced as the knots began to loosen and the circulation increased in her fingers. "This is connected to a case, isn't it?"

He shook his head. She had her back to him and she knew he'd done it. Was it a movement of the air, a rustle of his clothing? Or was it the connection they'd always shared? Even when they couldn't share their dreams or their heartbreaks.

"I'm not on a case right now. I'm trying to stick close to the ranch. Irina's not doing well. She's stopped searching for Rook."

"What? Oh, Deke. I can't believe she'd ever— Did she find out something?"

"Ran out of money." He pushed air out between his clenched teeth, a sure sign he was frustrated about something.

"She stopped because of *money?*"

"She either had to stop the search or fire at least two specialists and cut back on voluntary cases."

His fingers strained against hers as he picked at one of the knots. His breath hitched and he grunted quietly.

Mindy knew what he was feeling. His arms were tied behind his back, just like hers were, and she couldn't even imagine the pain in his wrists from working against the stiff ropes. She wanted to say something, to at least acknowledge the pain he was going through. But Deke Cunningham would never admit pain. Not pain. Not hurt. Not heartache.

"But Rook's her *husband.* I can't believe she'd quit for *any* reason. I'd never—" she stopped, biting her tongue—literally. *Never give up* was what she'd been about to say.

But she had. She'd given up on them.

"Well, she did." Deke's curt answer told her that he hadn't missed what she'd almost said. His breath hissed out between his teeth again. A sure sign that he was hurting.

Not knowing what else to say, she kept talking about Irina Castle. Maybe if he got irritated enough with her, it would distract him from the pain in his wrists.

"She must be devastated. It would be bad enough to

give up if she knew it was useless. But not to know, and to have to stop because of money. When did she make that decision?"

He didn't respond, just kept working silently.

He didn't want to tell her. Dear Lord, she knew him so well. "When, Deke?"

At that moment she felt the ropes give, releasing the strain on her shoulders, arms and wrists. Pain shot through her muscles as they relaxed. She bit her lip and tried to suppress a groan.

"Easy," Deke muttered. "Don't move too fast. You'll regret it, trust me."

It was one of the cryptic remarks that reminded her how little she knew about this man she'd loved as long as she could remember. She slowly flexed her arms and shoulders, clamping her jaw against the pain, as her brain filed that tidbit of information away with the others she'd collected over the years.

He knew how it felt to be tied up for hours—or days.

He twisted around. "Turn around this way. I need you to get my knife," he said. "It's in my left boot, *if* they didn't strip-search me while I was out. They took my gun. Thank God I ditched my cell phone."

She twisted awkwardly around until her shoulder bumped his. "They didn't search you after they brought you down here. They didn't have time. One of them got a phone call, but he obviously didn't want to talk in front of me, so they left." She looked down, but the tiny window didn't provide enough light for her to see that close to the ground. Still, she knew she couldn't bend over far enough to reach his boot.

"Good. See if you can grab my knife."

"No," she said flatly. "I can't."

"Come on, Min. It's sticking down in the side of my left boot. You remember where I keep it."

"I *can't.*"

"Why not?"

She bit her lip. She'd put off the *big reveal* as long as she could.

"Are you injured? Too stiff? What?"

She almost cried. He assumed she was hurting. And she let him think that. Dear heavens, she'd never realized what a coward she was.

"These knots are so slippery, I'll bet I can loosen them." He kicked his feet back and forth, working the ropes. "There." He inched around.

Mindy could see his head and shoulders in the dim light. She'd already felt the comforting softness and smelled the old-leather smell of his jacket. So it was no surprise that even with the darkness leaching the color out of everything, she could see the way it bunched across his constrained shoulders. She could even see the shadow of his too-long hair on the sheepskin collar.

He straightened his leg and barely missed brushing her tummy with the side of his boot. She flexed her cramped fingers and rubbed the indentations on her wrists. Then quickly, she wrapped her right arm around his calf and got her hands behind the boot heel and tugged.

"Pull your foot backward against my hands."

"You got it, sugar."

Her heart twisted until she wanted to cry out. "And don't call me sugar," she hissed.

He pulled backward, inadvertently pushing his heel into her tummy. "Hey—" he said.

Mindy cringed. "What?" she snapped.

"Have you gained weight?"

"Deke, this is serious."

He didn't say anything for a couple of seconds. "I know it is."

Tugging harder, she finally got a purchase on the boot heel and jerked it off his foot. His knife fell into her lap as something clattered against the crate and onto the floor.

"There," she said, breathing hard as she pushed his foot off her lap and picked up the knife. She pressed the button that sprung the blade. It snicked into place.

Deke jumped at the sound. "Hey, careful. It's sharp."

"I remember that, too." She slid the knife blade between his wrists. The blade sliced through the thick rope as if it were warm butter.

Deke carefully relaxed his shoulders and moved his arms. He grunted a couple of times.

She knew what he was going through. He hadn't been tied up as long as she had, but she figured the kidnappers hadn't been as careful with him as they had with her. His hands had to be on fire as the blood rushed back to them.

She handed him the knife, her heart pounding. When he leaned over to cut the ropes binding her feet, would he see why he'd gotten the impression she'd gained weight?

She held her breath while he cut the ropes. "I had a cigarette lighter in my boot with the knife. I think I heard it fall."

Mindy felt around with her foot until she touched a small cylinder. "Here it is." She kicked it toward him.

He grabbed it and sat up, grunting. "Whoa! I can understand why you didn't want to bend over. I'm still kind of woozy." He reached a hand out to the wall beside him and stood. His shadow loomed over her "Can you stand up? We need to get out of here."

Mindy crouched there, her shoulders hunched. Right now, he couldn't see anything. But as soon as she stood—

Dear God, please help me. When Deke sees me, I'm going to need all the courage you can spare.

He was about to find out that she was pregnant. She had no idea what he'd do.

She *did* remember what he'd said he'd do.

Years ago, when they were seventeen, she'd had a scare. She was late, and the pregnancy test had read positive. When she'd told Deke, his reaction had been immediate. Shock and abject terror had darkened his features.

You're pregnant? No. No way. You gotta do something. There's enough screwed-up Cunninghams in the world already.

She'd been stunned and frightened. But she'd understood. If she'd had the baby, Deke would be gone. But the issue was moot, because a few days later she'd started her period. They'd never spoken about it again.

Now here she was, six weeks away from bringing a Cunningham into the world. And six seconds away from Deke finding out.

"Stand up." He held out his hand. "You'll be woozy, but I won't let you fall."

Mindy sucked in a deep breath and took his hand. Struggling, bracing herself against the wall, and with a lot of grunting and groaning, she managed to push herself upright.

When their gazes met, his expression softened and his fingers tightened on her hand. "Hey, Min. It's been a long time." His mouth quirked.

She swallowed hard. "Long time," she replied, with a nervous nod.

"I'm so sorry they hurt you," he whispered. He leaned in closer, a gentle smile on his face.

Then he stopped—dead still. His gaze flickered downward.

Her mouth went dry. She couldn't move. All she could do was stand there.

She knew what he saw. A dark wool peacoat, navy blue pants and low-heeled boots. Pretty standard wear for this weather.

But the peacoat stuck out to *there,* and he'd just bumped into her tummy.

Her hands moved to cradle the baby. She couldn't stop them. It was an innate reaction, a protective instinct. Shielding her baby from what was to come.

Trembling with trepidation, she braced herself.

Deke stood frozen, his face lit by the fading beam of light from the tiny window. As wan and dim as the light was, she still saw the color drain from his face. His blue eyes widened and his mouth dropped open.

Mindy cradled her belly tighter.

"Min—?" His voice broke.

She bit her lip as her heart broke.

He shook his head as if to clear it—or to deny the truth before his eyes.

Then it hit—the storm of Deke's anger. His brows lowered until his eyes were dark and hooded. "Mindy, what the hell have you done?"

She tried to hold her own against Deke's fiery gaze, but she couldn't. She had to look away.

"Deke, that kidnapper is coming back anytime. It's been hours since he checked on me."

"I'll deal with him when he gets here." His voice was tight with what? Confusion? Shock? Fury? She couldn't sort out all the emotions. For the first time since she'd known him she wasn't sure what was behind his clipped words.

"How did you—?"

The baby kicked, probably feeling her distress. She rubbed the spot and he calmed down. "How? The usual way."

"So who's the lucky guy?"

And there it was. Deke Cunningham's patented defense system. More efficient than any antimissile missile the government had ever dreamed up. It was as effective and high-tech as the Starship *Enterprise*'s shields, and as quick to rise to protect his heart.

Although she understood why he did it, his words still hurt. She braced herself. "You are."

Chapter Three

Mindy sucked in a deep breath as she watched her ex-husband and waited for the explosion.

His face was still lit by that small rectangle of light. If he realized it, he'd move—cover his reaction with darkness. But right this second she had a unique opportunity to watch his face as he processed what she'd said.

His eyes widened in panic for a split second, then narrowed. His brows knit in a frown and he blew air out between his clenched teeth. "That's impossible. We haven't even seen each other in almost a year."

"Eight months plus a week, to be exact," she murmured.

"Eight—oh. Your mom's funeral." He shot her a look before he turned away, out of the wan spotlight. Then tightly, "Why didn't you tell me?"

"You know why. Look at your reaction. Now can we focus on the kidnapper, who's going to show up any minute?"

"Fine," he snapped. He wiped a hand down his face and around to rub the nape of his neck.

When he turned back around, his features were carefully neutral and his voice was all business. "What do you know about this place? Where's the door?"

She ignored his curt tone and pointed behind them. "There's a staircase back there. I hear the door open. I see light until he closes it. Then he comes down the stairs. Twelve. Twelve steps."

Deke tried to concentrate on her words. She was absolutely right. They needed to get out of there before their captors came back.

But all he could think about was her...condition. And she was right about his reaction. Years ago she'd come to him, worried that she might be pregnant, and he'd lost it. Yelled at her.

Scared her. His heart twisted with regret for an instant, then leapt again in renewed panic.

The idea of having a kid scared him. More than anything he'd ever come up against—before or since. And he'd faced a lot.

But a baby. His mouth went dry and his chest tightened.

Damn it, he didn't have time to be distracted by emotion. He had to focus. He squeezed his eyes shut and forced himself to concentrate on the danger. To forget that his ex-wife was carrying his child.

He growled under his breath and looked in the direction she'd indicated. He recognized the stairs. Their shape stood out as a darker shadow ascending into blackness.

The basement was so damn dark, and the light from the window above was waning. He was pretty sure, based on his instinctive sense of direction, that the window faced east.

He'd driven in from the east, from nearby Casper.

He wasn't sure what good that information did him, but at least he was oriented now.

"It's getting dark out. What else have you seen? Did the man bring a light with him?"

Mindy's hands were cradling her belly and her head was inclined. A serene expression made her face as beautiful as a Madonna. Amazingly, even in the darkness of the basement, she glowed. She was lush and beautiful. He wanted her so bad he ached.

Stop it!

She looked up, frowning. He could see her processing his words. "No. The last time, he and another guy were dragging you. I couldn't figure out what I was hearing until you grunted." She smiled. "No mistaking that growl. Anyhow, when they took off my blindfold I tried to take in as much as I could before they left and closed that door. I saw something over there, beyond that stack of wood. Maybe a door, or an opening of some kind."

"Stay right there," Deke ordered, pointing at her feet. He moved carefully toward the place she'd indicated. The entire floor was dirt, and littered with boards and logs along with pieces of broken furniture.

Within minutes it would be too dark to see, but his senses took in the shapes of the shadows and the musty smells. He figured that there was very little down here newer than fifty years old.

Finally, his outstretched hands touched the wall. Mindy was right. Complete darkness had already encroached on this end of the basement. He ran his hands over the rough-hewn boards. If there was a door, he couldn't find it.

He rapped on the wood, listening for a hollow echo. No luck. Every place he knocked sounded solid as a rock.

Finally, as a last resort, he reached in his pocket and pulled out the disposable cigarette lighter. He shook it. Fairly full. Striking it with his thumb, he used its light to quickly examine the wall.

"Deke?"

Mindy's scared voice, harsh with the strain of holding herself together, tore through him.

"Just a minute, sugar," he said, studying the crevices between the boards. If there was an opening in this alcove, he couldn't find it.

The lighter was beginning to burn his thumb, so he let go, then turned around and made his way back to her.

"Okay. I'm going upstairs and check things out. You stay here. You were right about the alcove, but I can't find a door anywhere, and we're almost out of light."

"Deke, you can't go up there. You said they wanted you to get out of the knots. That means they'll be waiting up there to ambush you."

"I'd be surprised if they weren't. But I'll deal with them. When I call you, we'll make a run for it."

Mindy shook her head. "No. It won't work. You can't—"

"Have you got a better idea? Because I don't. Our only other choice is to wait until they come back, and I'm not going to fight them down here so close to you. You could get hurt. Now give me my knife and stop arguing. You're wasting time. Nothing's going to happen to me."

"You don't know that—"

"Nothing ever has."

"We both know that's not true."

Deke clenched his jaw. The arguing had always come so easily. Just like the sex. Two things they'd always gotten right.

They'd learned early how to push each other's buttons.

"My knife, Mindy."

She handed it to him.

He closed it and stuck it in his pocket. Then he dropped the disposable lighter down inside his boot.

"Grab those ropes and sit back down. I'll wrap them loosely around your hands and feet, so you'll look like you're still tied up if they—" he paused "—get past me."

"Wait. I don't understand."

"If they come down here, I want you to look like you're still tied up. That way they can't blame you for trying to escape. Just me."

Mindy slowly bent down, reaching a hand out to steady herself against the wall.

Deke grimaced. This was going to be harder than he could have imagined. She was so handicapped by her pregnancy that she couldn't even bend down. He cupped her elbow.

"Okay, never mind." He led her over to sit on the wooden crate and fetched the ropes.

"Put your hands behind your back."

He took her hands and carefully looped the rope around them. Then, bending in front of her, he wrapped the second rope around her feet.

He straightened. "Good. In the dark, it'll look like you're really tied up."

"I *feel* like I'm really tied up. Are you sure about this?" Her voice was edged with panic.

"Trust me, sugar." His mouth flattened in a grimace, just like it did every time he said those words to her. She couldn't trust him. He knew it, and she knew it. He'd let her down too many times.

"But how—"

He placed into her palm one end of the rope that was wrapped around her hands. "Hang on to that end of the rope. When you pull it the ropes will fall off. The ropes around your feet aren't secured at all. Just kick them."

"Deke, I don't like this."

He glanced at the lone window, high above their heads. Then, closing his eyes, he formed a mental blueprint of the main floor of the hotel in his brain. "If the desk is there, and the stairs are there—" he muttered, tracing the most likely route out of the building.

"Listen to me, Min. That window faces east. My car is out there. Whatever you do, keep yourself oriented. The front of the building faces south." He pointed in that direction. "Which means these stairs are on the north side. That door probably opens into the kitchen."

He laid his palms against her shoulders. "Relax," he said, massaging the muscles there. "You can let your hands rest against the ropes. They won't give unless you jerk the end you have in your fingers."

"The dining room is through an arched doorway to the right—east—of the desk. I want you to wait down here until I call you. If you don't hear anything within a half hour, undo the ropes and run up the stairs. If you see a clear shot to a back door, take it. Otherwise run through the dining room into the lobby and hightail it out the front door."

"Hightailing is not so easy these days."

Deke grabbed her arm. "Listen to me, Min. Your life and the life of—" He couldn't say the words. "Whatever happens, you *have* to save yourself. Got it?"

She bit her lip and looked up at him. "Deke, I—"

"Got—it?" he bit out.

"G-got it."

"When you get to my car, you'll find a spare key and a cell phone under the driver's seat."

"Who's supposed to be there to help—?"

"Drive like hell due east. Call Irina. Her number is first on the call list."

Mindy stared at him, wide-eyed. On her face was a mixture of trust, fear, doubt and a shadow that didn't come from the dim light in the room. It came from inside her. Slowly, she nodded.

He turned toward the stairs and stopped.

He was leaving Mindy undefended. Mindy and his unborn child. A strange mixture of pride and abject terror weakened his knees.

He'd saved a lot of innocent lives, and while he understood that underestimating his enemy could be fatal, he'd never once doubted his own ability.

Okay—once. Right now, he felt like a rookie who'd been handed two equally deadly choices.

For the first time in his life, he hesitated over which course to take. For the *second* time ever, the awful consequences of failure slammed him in the face.

There was a reason Deke Cunningham never thought about losing. Because to consider the results was unbearable.

If he went out there armed with a four-inch switchblade, he had a very good chance of succeeding—against one or two, maybe even three opponents. But if he failed—

If he failed, he left Mindy and his child vulnerable. That was unthinkable.

He turned around. "Here's what I'm going to do," he said, stepping over to her and bending down until his lips were next to her ear. "Keep the knife."

She looked shocked. "But—"

"Shh."

"But Deke," she whispered. "That's your— No. I mean, no, you can't go out there with nothing."

He held out his hands in front of her face. "I've got these. Now, where do you want me to put the knife? In the pocket of your coat?"

She shook her head. "Everything I put in those slanted pockets falls out. Put it in my bra."

"Your—?"

"Shh." She smiled wryly. "It's not like you don't know where it is. Do you want me to do it? And then you can retie the ropes around my hands?"

He shook his head, rubbing his face against her silky, tangerine-scented skin. "I'll do it." He opened her coat and unbuttoned the three buttons at the neckline of her sweater, then he pulled the knife out of his pocket.

"Okay," he whispered, feeling like a kid about to cop his first feel. He felt that awkward, that shy, that excited.

Quickly he slid his hand down through the neckline of her sweater. When his fingers slid over the rising mounds of her breasts, he almost gasped. They were so full and round and firm.

Her body was preparing for her child. Awed and speechless, and working as fast as he could, he slid the knife between her breast and the cup of the bra.

"Does that feel okay?"

Her head inclined slightly. "It's good," she murmured, sounding a little breathless.

He extracted his hand and rebuttoned her sweater. Then he pulled the lapels of her coat together. When he lifted his gaze, she was looking up at him.

He wanted to kiss her so badly he ached. Not a lover's kiss. Just a gesture of caring, a promise that he'd do anything to protect her and the child that she sheltered inside her.

But he'd made her so many promises, and he'd broken them all.

So instead, he made a vow to himself. A simple vow. Yet one more difficult to keep than any promise he'd made to her, kept or not.

He vowed that when she was safe, he'd get out of her life and stay out. He grinned as pain stabbed his heart. Leaving her meant leaving his child. Still, she and the baby would be better off if he was out of their lives. And she knew it.

She deserved a chance to make a new life with her baby. The kind of life she'd always wanted but never had with him.

A normal, safe life.

"Ready, Min?" he whispered.

She lifted her chin and her eyes drifted shut. After a second, she opened them again. "I'm ready."

After one more tug on the lapels of her coat, he left her there and climbed the stairs. At the top, he turned around to check on her. He couldn't see her. Everything below him was a lake of darkness.

That was good.

He nodded in her direction, knowing she could see

him, then reached out toward the doorknob. His hand stilled just millimeters from the knob as qualms assailed him.

"Here we go, Min," he whispered. "Be ready for anything." He turned the doorknob carefully, repeating the warning to himself. Then he pushed open the door.

The room in front of him was nearly as shrouded in darkness as the basement below. He took a careful step forward as his eyes sought the source of the faint light he'd seen under the threshold. It seemed to be coming from behind the open door. Probably daylight from the dining room and lobby.

Without moving, he listened. *Nothing.* Still the uneasy feeling that had prickled his nape—the feeling that someone was watching—wouldn't leave him.

He took a step forward so he could pull the door shut behind him. A blinding bright light flared in front of his face.

He squeezed his eyes shut and whirled toward the light, swinging his clasped fists like a sledgehammer, hoping to take down whoever was holding it.

Fireworks exploded inside his head, snapping it backward. He grabbed at the doorknob, but his hand barely brushed it.

He managed to get his feet under him, even though the blow still rang in his head and his eyes were still blinded. He swung his fists, seeking a target, but just as he connected sidelong with what felt like an arm, something heavy and forceful hit him in the middle of his chest.

He fell backward through the open door. He managed to grab the stair rail, but it didn't hold. Nails screeched as the wood gave way. He heard a scream. *Mindy?*

His butt bumped down a couple of stairs before he managed to stop himself.

He still couldn't see, but over the years he'd honed all his senses. Now they came to his aid as he reacted instinctively, like an animal.

He heard a heavy step on the hollow stairs, felt the swish of air that indicated movement close to him.

He scrabbled to get his feet under him and prepared to launch himself at his attacker. Before he could do more than tense his thighs to spring, a dark figure loomed in his blurry vision and swung something shiny at his head.

MINDY KNEW SCALP WOUNDS BLED a lot. That was Nursing 101, but she'd been an administrator for so long she'd forgotten a lot of the everyday side of nursing, like how bad a little bit of blood could appear.

The cut on Deke's forehead wasn't little. An inch-long diagonal slice was laid open above his right eyebrow, and he looked like he'd lost a fistfight with a heavyweight.

The guy standing over him wouldn't have made middleweight soaking wet. He was medium height and skinny, and dressed as if he'd stepped out of a B Western, down to the curled-brim black hat and the red bandanna tied over his nose and mouth. He still clutched the big six-gun he'd used to coldcock Deke.

As she watched, he cautiously nudged Deke's ribs with a silver-toed cowboy boot.

Deke stirred and groaned.

The man jerked his foot away.

Mindy held her breath, trying her best to stay still. She'd almost given herself away by jumping up when Deke tumbled down the stairs. She *had* screamed at him.

He'd rounded on her and warned her in a gruff, fake Texas drawl that if she didn't shut up he'd stuff a rag in her mouth and blindfold her. She'd nodded meekly and stayed as still as her worry and agitation would let her.

"Get up, Cunningham," the gunman growled. He stood over Deke, watching him warily, one hand pointing his gun and the other resting on what looked like a stubby billy club. "You think you're pretty smart, don't you? Getting yourself untied. How come you didn't untie your girlfriend? Oh, wait. She's your wife, ain't she? Or is that your ex-wife?"

Deke pushed himself up to his hands and knees and shook his head, slinging droplets of blood in a semicircle around him.

"Min?" he rasped.

At that instant the cowboy reared back and kicked him in the gut. He dropped with a pained grunt.

Despite her resolve, Mindy gasped aloud.

Deke's grunt stretched out into a growl. He bowed his back and dropped his head.

She watched in stunned awe as he got his feet under him and sprang up like a big cat. He hurled himself at the gunman.

The gunman barely sidestepped in time to avoid being bowled over. Deke checked his lunge, twisting and falling on his shoulder.

The man turned toward Mindy, pressing the barrel of the gun into her temple. "Don't make another move," he yelled. "I'll kill her. She's disposable now that I've got you."

"Stop!" Deke shouted, as he rolled and shot to his feet. His hands spread in a gesture of surrender. "What do you want? Just tell me what you want."

Don't, Mindy wanted to cry. *Don't give in to his scare tactics.* But even if she could have spoken, she was too terrified to put up a brave front. She was terrified—for herself, yes, but more for the baby.

She closed her fist around the piece of rope in her hand, wishing she could figure out a way to surprise the gunman.

Something of what she was thinking must have shown in her face, because Deke shook his head, a subtle movement worthy of a major league pitcher refusing his catcher's signal.

Meanwhile, the gunman thumbed his ridiculous hat up onto his forehead. His little beady eyes crinkled. The red bandanna tied around his nose and mouth stretched, suggesting a grin.

"Whadda I want?" he growled in his silly Texas accent. "I want answers—"

"Fine," Deke broke in, spreading his hands wider. "Let Mindy go, and I'll give you all the answers you could possibly want. Fire away."

The man shook his head slowly from side to side. "Not yet. If I ask you now, you'll just lie to me. I figure it'll take a couple days to wear you down," he drawled. "By then you'll have tried everything you can think of to escape or get the drop on me, and you'll fail every time. You'll be hungry and thirsty and tired. Even better, your gal there'll be pretty darn sick from hunger and exhaustion, seeing as how she's *that* close to whelpin' that pup. It yours?"

"That's none of your damn business. Who the hell are you anyhow?"

"So it ain't yours." He chuckled nasally. "She been sleeping around on you, ain't she?"

Deke went still. Mindy knew he was about two seconds from a firestorm.

"Deke—" she said quietly.

He shushed her with a wave of his hand and lowered his head. His dark eyes glowed dangerously. "Who are you?" he growled.

Mindy watched his fingers curl—not into fists. They curved like claws, ready to sink into the soft flesh of the man's neck. His knees bent slightly, like a cat about to spring.

The gunman took a half step closer to Mindy's side and pressed the gun barrel into her flesh. "I'm asking the questions here, Cunningham. You'll find out who I am soon enough. Meanwhile, you can call me Frank James." He chuckled. "Now it's time for you to get a taste of what's to come."

"You come near me again, you'll regret it for a long time."

The bandanna stretched again, and the black eyes crinkled. "Don't worry, Cunningham. I'm not planning to come near you. Not right now."

He cocked his weapon slowly, drawing out the *snick-snick* of metal against metal. Mindy felt the end of the barrel scrape against her skin.

Deke's head jerked slightly and his face drained of color. "Wait!" he snapped.

She closed her eyes involuntarily, and her shoulders tensed.

"Wanna play a game? How about Russian roulette? How about you Mrs. Ex-Cunningham?"

"Put the gun down," Deke warned. He stepped forward, his hands still out, and still curved like claws.

Mindy pulled the end of the rope Deke had left in

her hand. Just as he'd promised her, the ropes immediately loosened and dropped silently to the floor. She had no idea what having her hands loose would do for her chances. But if an opportunity presented itself, she planned to be ready.

"Don't move!" Frank James shouted. Coward that he was, he moved behind Mindy, and put one hand against the side of her head while he pressed the barrel into her temple with the other.

Deke hadn't taken his eyes off James since the instant he'd cocked his gun. His expression was a mask of fear and nausea. He believed Frank James would shoot her.

The realization of how afraid Deke was sent panic fluttering into her throat.

Right now they were in a standoff. Deke couldn't rush James without fear that he'd pull the trigger. James couldn't easily lower his gun without the fear that Deke might jump him. And she couldn't do anything.

Or could she?

Her hands were free, and James didn't know that. Considering his position, if she interlaced her fingers to form a double fist, she might be able to slam him in the groin and get away.

Okay, maybe not get away—not constrained by her bulk as she was. But at least she could give Deke a chance to jump him while he was doubled over with pain. Maybe Deke could even grab his gun.

Of course she could also get herself shot in the head. But at least she'd be shot trying to do something. Frank James didn't sound like the most stable kidnapper on the planet. He could accidentally pull the trigger at any second.

Here goes. She looked up at Deke and slowly winked at him. His brows drew down slightly. He gave her another of his World Series-caliber head shakes.

But she couldn't obey him. She had to try something. With excruciating slowness she pushed her fingers together, moving her shoulders as little as possible.

She moaned loud enough for James to hear her as she drew up carefully, until every muscle and tendon in her arms and shoulders were tense and poised, preparing for one ultimate purpose—driving her fists into Frank James's groin.

"Shut up," he snapped.

"But I'm hurting." She made her voice small and hesitant. "I need to move my legs. Please?"

James made a growling sound in his throat, but he eased off the pressure of the barrel at her temple.

Mindy shifted position, using the movement to brace her feet on the floor. Then she took a long, slow breath, and sighed, as if in relief.

Deke's body tensed expectantly. At that instant, she rammed her fists backward, putting all her weight and all her determination behind the blow.

She connected.

James squealed and dropped his gun.

Deke dove forward.

Mindy froze, staying as still as possible. She felt Deke's hands sliding under her arms. He lifted her up off the crate and out of the way.

But by the time he'd turned back to James, the man had retrieved the short baton from his belt. He flicked his wrist and it telescoped.

Deke stopped in midlunge and backpedaled. He held up his hands, palms out, and glanced back her way.

James flicked his thumb and a faint crackling hum filled the air.

Mindy stiffened. What *was* that thing?

Then he lunged, as if with a fencing sword, right for Deke's solar plexus. Deke tried to pull back, but she was too close behind him, so he took the full brunt of the attack. His spine arched sharply and he growled between clenched teeth. Then he flopped to the ground like a discarded rag doll.

Chapter Four

"Deke!" Mindy screamed, as he collapsed to the dirt floor of the basement. "What did you do to him?"

"Shut up, honey, or I'll give you a dose of the same."

She cradled her belly and glared at Frank James, or whatever the heck his name was. She was so damn helpless.

I love you, Sprout, but you're crippling me.

Deke heard Mindy's scream, but he couldn't make sense of what she'd said. He had to get to her.

Cold dirt scraped against his cheek.

What the hell was the ground doing there?

He tried to lift a hand, but his hand wasn't paying attention to his brain. Nor were his feet. Even his eyelids seemed stuck open.

He saw a movement in front of his eyes. Something glittery—silver? James's damn cowboy boots. Fake and all show, just like the lowlife who was wearing them.

Kick me again, bastard, and I'll make you regret it. At least that was what he wanted to say, but his mouth wasn't cooperating, either.

From somewhere he smelled the aroma of tangerines, mingled with dirt, mildew and the faint odor of burnt hair.

Then, more static filled his ears, his muscles spasmed in unbelievable pain and lightning struck his head.

WHEN HE GOT BACK TO HIS ROOM it was almost midnight. The strategy meeting Irina had called had lasted a lot longer than planned, mostly because they couldn't agree on a course of action.

He'd tried to sound helpful but neutral. Trouble was, everybody else was doing the same thing. Ultimately the only decision that was agreed upon was that Irina would not leave Castle Ranch until the threat from Novus Ordo was over.

He could see in the other guys' eyes that they were as skeptical as he was that she'd be able to stay put that long.

He bolted his door and put the chain on, made sure the blinds were closed, then went into the bathroom and dug in his shaving kit for the miniature cell phone.

Sure enough—a missed call. Reluctantly, he pressed the callback button, wishing he had good news to report.

THE INSIDE OF DEKE'S EYELIDS screamed with pain.

It was that damn sand. It got into everything. Slowly, he opened his eyes to a narrow slit. The tent was dark, so he had a few hours before Novus's man came to torture him again.

He came every day. Every damn day. With that laugh. That gun.

That sound.

An icy shudder of helpless terror crawled up his spine as he relived those awful few seconds. They never varied.

First, the pressure of cold steel against his temple. Then the split second of screaming panic and soul-wrenching sorrow before the hammer clicked against the empty chamber.

The sound triggered a cold sweat of relief, and the casually curious question of whether he would hear that same clicking sound if the hammer impacted a live round.

Finally came the regret that he'd lived through one more day. Because that meant tomorrow he'd have to face the same fate again. The inside of his mouth turned to sand-blown desert.

Taking a deep breath and cringing against the anticipated agony of his dislocated shoulders, he moved. Pain shrieked through him, but not the pain he'd expected.

What the hell? He hurt everywhere—not just his shoulders. His hands weren't even bound behind his back.

Something had changed. But why? He'd been in this hell called Mahjidastan so long he'd lost count of the days. The predictability, the inevitability, had become as torturous as the pain and fear.

He carefully lifted his head, which hurt like a sonofabitch. Taking a cautious breath, he coughed.

Dirt, mildew, old wood—completely different from the stink of urine and camel dung he'd expected. This wasn't Mahjidastan, the tiny disputed province in the region where Afghanistan, Pakistan and China joined.

He opened his eyes. Not easy. They were matted with

dried blood and caked with dust. Blinking and wincing as he stretched his sore neck tendons, he lifted his head again, even more cautiously this time, and looked around.

Slowly, his brain gathered up his scattered, disorganized memories.

He was in a ghost town, in the basement of an abandoned hotel. He'd come here to rescue Mindy. *Mindy and their unborn baby.*

He stiffened at that thought, causing his muscles to seize in bone-cracking pain, bending him double. With a superhuman effort, he unclenched his fists. Holding his breath, he stretched his legs. As long as he moved with unbearable slowness, the spasms stayed away—for the most part.

Frank James had slugged him, kicked him and then Tasered him.

"Mindy!" he croaked. The last thing he'd seen was James holding that damn gun at her head. The sight had come closer to breaking him than anything he'd ever faced in his life. Because he knew the dread, the fear—the sound of that hollow click. He would give his life if it meant that Mindy never had to experience that.

Immediately, that image was replaced by another one. The image of shock and agony on James's face when Mindy hit him in the groin.

Deke chuckled, which knotted his neck muscles and sent a painful spasm through them. That was his Mindy. She'd acted with the ingenuity and determination that had made him love her from the moment he'd first laid eyes on her when they were ten years old.

Then reality sheared his breath. Where was she? Had that weaselly coward Tasered her? Had he hurt their baby?

He'd kill him with his bare hands if he had.

By moving slowly and stopping when a twinge foreshadowed a muscle spasm, he got his feet under him. Damn, but everything hurt.

He'd been Tasered before, in training. But that was nothing compared to this. He spread his fingers carefully. The amount of voltage Frank James had used could do serious damage. Hell, it could kill. The spasms caused by the electric shock could stop the heart.

He had to find Mindy, make sure she was all right.

He leaned against the wall as his knees threatened to buckle and his head spun dizzily. Bile burned in his throat, and nausea sent acrid saliva flowing into his mouth.

He forced himself to think rationally. Chronologically. First things first. How long had he been unconscious?

He looked at the shadows on the floor. Light was coming in from somewhere above and behind him. He turned his head, squinting through his aching eyes.

That window. He recognized it. He was still in the hotel's basement. The way the light streamed in, and its bright yellow color, told him it was daylight—morning. At least he could see better than he'd been able to last night.

There were the crates they'd been sitting on, and in a tangle on the dirt floor were the ropes that had bound them.

"Mindy!" he croaked, then stopped and listened.

Nothing. A knot of fear tightened in his gut. "Mindy, sugar? You've got to answer me. Where are you?"

If that ridiculous cowboy had hurt her—

Frank James had to be working for Novus Ordo. It was the only thing that made sense, given everything that had led up to this point.

"Damn you, Novus!" he growled. "This is your doing. I know it."

He knew Novus and Novus knew him. It was Novus who'd had his helicopter shot down during a covert rescue mission over northern Mahjidastan. Who'd had him tortured, made him reveal how he had found his camp, and how he knew Novus was holding Travis Ronson, the only son of Wyoming senator Frederick Ronson. The senator had been a great friend of Rook's dad, and Travis, who was a journalist with the Associated Press, had disappeared while embedded with American troops in Afghanistan.

Rook had come after Deke in the middle of a windstorm. That's when he'd gotten a look at Novus's bare face without the famous surgical mask he always wore.

Novus knew him—knew that no matter what he did to him, Deke would never break. He also knew the lengths Rook and Deke would go to in order to rescue each other.

So all this, the cleverly tied ropes, the near escape, were Novus's revenge on Deke for escaping and his proof that he was stronger and smarter than Deke.

He was toying with him, like a cat with a mouse. Waiting for him to break.

It didn't make sense to Deke that a man with a goal of destroying the United States would spend time toying with a man just for revenge. Didn't he have better things to do? Like achieve world domination?

Now, he'd taken Mindy away again and left Deke to

find her. It was a deadly game of hide-and-seek—with life or death hanging in the balance.

He knew Novus Ordo was a smart guy. He hadn't gotten to be the most feared terrorist on the planet by being sloppy. He'd worked fast and smart to get this complex plan in place in the week since Irina had stopped the search for Rook.

He'd lured Deke here by using Mindy as bait. It was exactly what Deke should have expected. He'd said as much to Irina two days ago.

"You surprised Novus when you suddenly called Matt back from Mahjidastan. He knew he had no chance of getting to you through all your security, so he targeted Matt first, figuring the reason you stopped was because Matt had found him. But Matt outsmarted his man."

Irina had nodded as Deke went on. "So Novus goes after the next obvious target. Me." He'd ground his fist into his other palm in frustration.

"He knows if anybody has information about whether Rook is still alive, I do. So he approaches it the easiest and most logical way, just like he did with Matt. He goes for the most bang for his buck. With Matt, it was his best friend's baby. With me, it's Mindy."

"Your Achilles' heel," Irina said matter-of-factly.

The three words echoed in his brain. She'd hit the nail square on the head. Mindy was his weakness.

His only weakness.

He'd promised Mindy he'd save her. And he would. He may have broken promises before, but he couldn't break this one. If he did, Mindy would die.

He licked dry lips as his gaze roamed around the basement, studying the layout. He hadn't gotten a chance to search the whole thing last night. There might be other alcoves or secret doors.

Before he'd headed out alone for Cleancutt, he'd spent as much time as he dared studying maps and satellite photos of the area.

His heart had sunk when he realized the call had come from an abandoned coal-mining town. A big one. It was one of the few that had actually grown rather than died around 1950 when underground coal mining had given way to strip-mining.

So it made sense that some of the newer buildings, like the hotel, had been built over old mining tunnels. It was highly likely that this basement connected to at least one of them.

Pushing away from the wall, he took a step, relieved that his muscles were no longer spasming, although they still trembled. So he concentrated on putting one foot in front of the other, taking it easy until he could be sure his knees wouldn't collapse.

He started his search of the basement under the window. It was the best-lit area and therefore the easiest to search.

He examined every wall, every nook and cranny, holding to his grid pattern. Finally he ended up on the far west side, where he'd looked for a door the night before.

In the dim daylight, he saw that the timbers lining the wall of the alcove looked different from the wood on the other walls. In fact, they looked like a door, except there was no handle.

He rapped on the wood with his knuckles. Yep. Solid as a rock. Cursing to himself, he moved his hand a few inches and rapped again.

His instincts had always been excellent, and combining that with the maps he'd studied and the local history of the area, he figured this was the most likely place for a door into the mine.

The mine he wasn't even sure was there.

Just as he moved his fist another few inches, preparing to rap again, he heard something. He froze, his knuckles millimeters from the rough wood. Closing his eyes, he listened.

There it was again. A faint rapping—muffled, barely audible.

He rapped again. And again heard the muffled answering rap.

"Mindy?" he called softly.

Nothing.

He drew a breath to yell, then paused. What if Frank James heard him? Yeah? So what? He'd bet money this was part of Novus's cat-and-mouse game, anyhow.

As he prepared to knock, the muffled rapping began again.

"I'm here, Min. Where are you?"

Was he projecting or, worse, hallucinating? He had to believe he'd really heard her. If she was on the other side of the wall, then there was a way through it. And he'd find it.

He rapped on every square inch of the alcove wall, starting at the top. The sound remained flat and solid.

He stopped again and listened.

There it was again. The answering rap. It didn't sound like she was knocking on the same wall he was.

"Mindy! Can you hear me? Is there a door?" He kept on, testing every inch of the wall. When he got down to knee level, he sat on his heels, wincing as his knees trembled and his leg muscles protested.

He knocked again. And got a different sound. A hollow sound.

Yes! His pulse pounded, sending pain arcing behind his eyes. *Damn Taser.*

"Mindy?" he called.

He heard something! A faint low murmur. It was her. He knew it.

Immediately, doubt sliced through him. What if it wasn't Mindy? What if it was another trap designed to wear him down?

Then he'd crawl right into it. He wasn't about to ignore even the smallest chance that Mindy was on the other side of the wall, counting on him to save her.

He examined the boards with his eyes and fingers. If he had to, he'd break it down with his bare hands to get to her.

He couldn't see anything unusual, but he sure as hell felt something. A slight difference in temperature—a slight movement of the air. Digging the lighter out of his pocket, he thumbed it.

Sure enough, the flame wavered. There was air behind the rough planks.

After a few frustrating seconds of digging at the corners of the boards, he thought of his knife. He reached toward his boot and then remembered. He didn't have it.

It was inside Mindy's bra. A thrill slid through him as he thought about how warm it would be from the heat of her body. He shook his head.

"Get out of my head," he muttered under his breath, and focused on digging out all that wood putty with his fingernails.

A long time later, with his fingertips scraped and sore, he called out to Mindy again.

"Mindy, if you can hear me, move back. I'm going to kick these boards in." He banged on the wall with his fist. "Right here. Okay?"

A faint tap answered him.

He sat back and drew his knees up to his chest.

"Okay," he hollered. "On three. One—two—"

He braced himself with his hands behind him. "Three!" He slammed the heels of his boots into the planks as hard as he could. The thud echoed through the basement.

Propelling himself forward, he examined the damage. *Not much.* "Min, stay back."

He rocked backward and stomped the wood again, and again. The fourth time it gave, with nails screeching as they separated from wood. Although his legs quivered with fatigue and reaction to the Taser, he kicked at the splintered wood until he'd opened a hole big enough to crawl through.

For a few seconds he sat quietly, listening. Had the deafening noise alerted Frank James? He waited, but nobody came.

If the fake cowboy wasn't sitting back watching his efforts through a hidden camera, Deke was certain he was listening and waiting, and probably laughing at Deke's efforts.

Lying down on the dirt floor, he peered through the opening, which was barely wide enough for his shoulders. "Mindy?" he whispered.

No answer.

He eased a bit farther in, holding his breath.

It could still be a trap.

A movement at the corner of his vision drew his eye. He tensed.

"Deke—?"

He clamped his jaw against the flood of relief that closed his throat and stung his eyelids.

She was there. And her voice sounded strong. But it was still undercut by that same terrified, desperate tone he'd noticed on the telephone. At the time he'd known something was horribly wrong, but he hadn't known what. Now he did.

She was afraid for her baby.

"Everything okay in there?"

"Yes," she answered.

"You alone?"

"Yes."

She sounded terrified. He hoped she was telling the truth. Once, he'd been able to tell by the timbre of her voice. Could he still?

What would he do if Frank James had her?

Nothing different. He was making himself vulnerable to attack by crawling through the small trapdoor, but he didn't have a choice. If he were alone, he'd reconnoiter, figure out the best place to defend his back and ambush his enemy.

But he wasn't alone. He had to get to Mindy.

"Stay back. I'm coming through." He ducked his head and slithered through the hole, then stood. It was damn dark in here. Darker than the basement with its tiny window. He wished he had something more than a disposable lighter.

Deke could barely make out her silhouette. "Min, honey? Are you okay? Are you alone? Did he hurt—"

Suddenly a firm, round tummy collided with him, and slender but strong arms wrapped around his waist. "Deke, I was so scared. I was afraid he'd killed you."

Deke's throat seized. He swallowed hard against the lump that suddenly grew there. Carefully, feeling as if he might break her if he squeezed too hard, he wrapped his arms around her shoulders.

She laid her head in the hollow between his neck and shoulder—her favorite place to sleep, she'd always told him.

"Nah," he croaked, then had to stop and clear his throat. "You know me. Nothing can break me. I'm fine. What about you? He didn't Taser you, did he?"

Mindy clung to Deke for dear life. If she could crawl inside him she would. Body to body, especially through clothes, wasn't enough. No matter how many times she'd feared for Deke's safety, even his sanity, she'd always known he would never hurt her. She'd always felt safe with him.

Almost always.

She hugged him tighter. His strong arms tightened around her—a little. He was holding back. Partly because he was still stunned and angry about her pregnancy, she was sure.

But that wasn't the whole reason. In all the time she'd known him, he'd never opened up to her—not completely.

She knew him so well—probably better than anybody alive. So she knew there was a deep core to Deke Cunningham that she'd never been able to penetrate.

She would bet a lot of money that nobody ever had. Or would. It broke her heart. It was the one thing she'd wanted from him that he'd never been able to give her—his complete trust. It was one of the reasons she'd finally given up and gotten a divorce.

"Min?"

She shook her head against the soft cotton of his shirt. "He didn't hurt me."

"How'd you get here? Can you find your way back?"

"I'm not sure. He blindfolded me again and we walked—it felt like hours. When he left me here it was so dark. I don't know how long I've stood here. I was afraid to sit down." She shuddered.

"That's right. You're pretty paranoid about creepy-crawlies, aren't you?" She felt his chest rumble with soft laughter.

"Don't laugh at me. And no. Not this time. I was so tired I'd have gladly sat in a nest of cockroaches. But I was afraid I wouldn't be able to get back up."

"Sorry." The amusement was gone. "Tell me everything you remember. Did you have to crawl through anything? Bend over to get through a door?"

"No. We went upstairs and then down again—twice. I think he was trying to confuse me. But once we went outside, I think into a different building. Then down a different set of stairs. Did you come from where we were tied up?"

"Yep. The old hotel. How'd you keep up with which building you were in?"

"Mostly by smell. The building we were in smells like mildew. The other one—wherever it was—had more of a smoky odor to it."

"Good! We might be able to find our way out by following our noses." Deke bent his head and kissed her forehead.

His lips moving against her skin took her back to those innocent high school days, when they'd been good together. Before they were old enough to understand that love alone couldn't always conquer fear or fill the hollow places left inside by an uncaring parent.

"You've got dried blood all over your face." She brushed at his temple and cheek, then ran the pad of her thumb gently across his closed eyelid. "And that cut needs to be washed and bandaged." She touched the skin around the cut and he winced. "Plus, you're going to have a bruise on your forehead."

"Yeah? Well, it'll match the rest of them."

Tears stung her eyes and she squeezed the lids shut. "You getting hurt is not funny to me." She pushed away from him.

He let go immediately.

When he did, she swayed. She knew what was wrong. She was tired. She was hungry. The *baby* was hungry. He got so restless when she didn't eat. "I need food."

"So what's new?"

"I mean for the baby."

He stiffened. "Oh. Yeah." He straightened and looked around. "Got any idea which way you came in?"

"I think we came from somewhere back there." She gestured toward a heavy wooden door on the north wall. "But I could be totally turned around."

"Okay." He wrapped his fingers around her upper arms and set her gently away from him. "Do you still have my knife? He didn't search you, did he?"

"No." She unbuttoned her sweater, retrieved the knife from her bra and handed it to him.

He closed his fist around it, soaking up her warmth. "You stay right there. I want to explore a little."

"Don't leave me," she breathed. She clutched at his white shirt. "If I lose you in the dark, I'll go crazy."

"You'll be fine. I'm not going far."

"Deke, what if he's waiting for you again?"

"I'll be ready for him. You stay right there."

Holding his knife in his right hand, he fished out the cigarette lighter with his left and struck it, then took a second to get his bearings. The trapdoor he'd come through was on the west wall of the basement. So he turned south, following the dirt wall until it curved around to the west. From the hollow sound of his footsteps and the whisper of air in his ears, he figured he was in a tunnel.

He walked a few feet farther, but nothing changed. The tunnel looked totally abandoned beyond the tiny circle of light cast by his lighter.

After extinguishing the lighter and pocketing it, he blindly examined the walls, but all he felt were thick, rough boards, like railroad ties, and dirt walls. In a few places his fingers brushed across some sort of mesh screening, probably designed to hold the dirt in place.

He felt along the ground with his feet, from wall to wall, but found nothing. No rails for the coal cars. This tunnel had probably never been finished. It was a dead end.

He retrieved the lighter and struck it again as he turned to retrace his steps. He'd felt steel rails under his boots in the alcove where Mindy was waiting. The rails led into the tunnel on the north side of the alcove. That was their only hope of getting out.

Just as he rounded the curve, back to the area where he'd left Mindy, light flared, revealing two dark silhouettes. Deke smelled the phosphorus smell of a match and the unmistakable odor of lantern oil. Alarm pierced his chest.

James. He had Mindy.

"Mindy?" He cautiously pressed his right arm against his side, hoping to conceal his knife. He didn't want to take a chance that James would catch a glint from the steel blade.

"Howdy, Cunningham," Frank James drawled. "Nice of you to join us. I've been waiting for you."

He hung an oil lantern on a nail above their heads with one hand, while his other aimed a Colt .45 revolver directly at Mindy's head. The red bandanna across his face stretched as he grinned.

Terror sheared Deke's breath for a second time. Previously, when he'd seen the steel barrel pressed against her temple, he'd sworn that if it killed him, James would never again get her into that life-or-death situation.

But here they were. And just like before, his consciousness was split in two. Half saw her precious head, once again threatened by the 9 mm barrel with its lethal cargo. The other half spun through a whirlwind of memories—the hot metal cylinder pressed against his own skull, the distinctive *snick-snick* of the hammer cocking, the slow grind of the barrel turning, and finally, the hollow click as it hit the empty chamber.

He knew the horror of waiting to hear those sounds. A shudder rocked his whole body.

He shook his head and stared at her. He had to stay here, in the present, on alert.

Her wide green eyes sparkled with tears as her hands cradled her tummy. "Deke, I didn't know—"

"Shut up!" James yelled.

Deke wanted to reassure her with his gaze, but he didn't think he could pull it off. So he turned his attention to James so she wouldn't see how scared he was that the man might be dumb enough to actually shoot her.

His only chance was to distract James and turn his anger toward him and away from Mindy.

"You're a coward," Deke growled. "Hiding behind a woman—a *pregnant* woman."

"You better watch yourself, pardner. You're not the one in charge here."

"In charge? Are you saying you are? Give me a break. You don't even have the guts to use your real name. You're named after an outlaw—hell! Not even a real outlaw. You're named after the *brother* of an outlaw."

Frank's eyes narrowed and his gun hand shook. "You shut up. Frank James was a great outlaw. As great as his brother."

Deke felt triumphant and apprehensive at the same time. He'd gotten to him. He'd struck a vein with the remark about the cowboy's moniker.

The guy was obviously under somebody's thumb. Most likely Novus. Frank was exactly what he looked like. A hired gun.

"Yeah, not so much. The only thing I remember about Frank James is that when people talk about Jesse they sometimes say, 'and Frank, too.' I know something else, too. I know you're ashamed of something or else you wouldn't be wearing that ridiculous bandanna over your face like a bad TV cowboy."

"You don't know anything about me." A red spot appeared in the center of James's forehead. And his gun hand shook.

That scared Deke. Nobody could trust a nervous

gun hand. Still, he had no choice. Somehow, he had to catch the guy off guard. All he needed was two seconds.

"I know enough to know you couldn't pull this off alone. You're working for Novus Ordo, aren't you?"

The gun barrel shook even more at the mention of the terrorist. "Shut up! You think you know so much. You don't know nothing." Dark spots dotted the bandanna where sweat rolled down James's pinched face.

Deke shifted to the balls of his feet and curled his fingers, ready to attack. *One second.* He only needed one second.

The cowboy was breathing hard, practically gasping, and the bandanna was fast becoming soaked. He looked like he was on the verge of panic.

Deke concentrated on keeping his own breathing even as he studied the other man. He'd bet money—hell, he was betting his life and Mindy's and her unborn baby's—that the coward had never killed anybody.

At least not face-to-face.

He could do this. He was bigger, stronger and faster. He *could* stop James before he got off a shot.

He had to.

As if he sensed Deke's resolve, James looked him dead in the eye. His beady pupils gleamed with malice as he cocked the hammer. He turned his head toward Mindy, still holding Deke's gaze.

Then his finger squeezed the trigger.

Chapter Five

Horror closed Deke's throat as he watched James's finger tighten on the trigger.

The sound of metal sliding against metal made him cringe. The chamber slowly turned.

Knowing he could never beat the bullet, and propelled by terror, Deke slung his knife underhanded at the cowboy's arm, then lunged at him with full-body force.

All hell broke loose.

Mindy screamed.

James squealed as Deke slammed into his skinny torso, pushing him against the timbers that lined the mine shaft. Gravel and dirt rained on their heads and peppered the dusty floor.

Deke shouldered James in the solar plexus as hard as he could. They crashed against the wall, and James's breath whooshed out. Deke closed his left hand around James's right wrist and beat it against the timbers, again and again.

Finally, the gun thudded to the dirt floor.

"Grab the gun, Min, or kick it away." He drove his forearm into James's face, trying to crush his nose and slam it up into his brain. James grunted and tried to shove Deke off him, but Deke wasn't about to let go.

He fisted his hands in James's shirt and dragged him forward, then body-slammed him against the wall again.

"Mindy!" he yelled.

She didn't answer.

Terrified that she was hurt, he threw the cowboy down to the ground, slamming his face into one of the steel rails, and whirled.

"Mindy!"

The oil lantern's flickering light sent shadows chasing around the tunnel. But none of them looked like her. Deke blinked as he scanned the small space.

"Deke—"

A wave of relief washed over him, so sharp, so spine-tingling, that it almost drove him to his knees. He turned toward her voice and saw a shadow move.

"Min," he breathed. She was on the ground. "Are you hurt?" He reached for her.

"I don't think so." She wrapped her arms around his neck as he lifted her.

"Stay back," he whispered, and set her gently against the far wall.

Her eyes slid past him and widened in the flickering lantern light. "Look out!"

When he whirled, Frank James was diving for the gun.

Deke dove, too, landing on top of the smaller man. He shoved him out of the way and reached out to grab the gun.

When he did, a searing pain slashed up his arm. Shocked, he fell backward.

Behind him, Mindy cried out.

He rolled and dove for the gun again, but it wasn't there.

James had it.

Deke was on the ground and James was standing, so he wrapped his arms around the silver-toed boots and jerked, hoping to knock James off his feet. Deke got his right foot under him for momentum and stability, but when he threw himself forward to unbalance James, his foot slipped.

He tried again and managed to head-butt James in the stomach. The man's breath whooshed out as he tumbled backward.

A thrill of triumph filled Deke's chest. He spotted the gleam of the knife blade at James's feet. He lunged for it.

At the very instant his fingers closed around its hilt, the heavy wooden door behind James opened and a big shadow loomed in the doorway.

Deke tried to check his momentum, but his feet slipped again. As if in slow motion, he saw the blue-white arc of the Taser coming at him.

MINDY WATCHED IN HORROR as a large, dark man appeared from nowhere. The light was behind him, so he was barely more than a silhouette, but she saw the blue light and heard the static.

The Taser.

Helpless to do anything, she merely stared as Deke's spine arched and the fine muscles hidden under his smooth, golden skin trembled. Then he dropped where he stood, his legs collapsing as if they'd turned into rags.

Then the big man kicked him out of the way. "Where's the woman?"

Deke had set her against the far wall, in the shadows. But she knew they'd spot her any second. There was no way she could defend herself, so instinctively, she closed her eyes and pretended to be unconscious.

"I don't know," James gasped, struggling to breathe. He coughed. "Forget her."

"Here she is."

Mindy's muscles tensed, and it was all she could do to keep from cringing.

"Leave her!" James yelled breathlessly.

She heard the bigger man's footsteps, felt him standing over her. She didn't know why she thought it was so important to keep up the pretense that she'd passed out, but she did.

"She's out cold. I can grab her."

"No! What did I just say?"

"But they could get away."

James's breathing was almost back to normal. "Get over here," he ordered.

Mindy heard the man's heavy footsteps recede.

"Now pay attention," James whispered.

She held her breath, listening.

"They're not going to get away. This isn't about capturing them. They're already captured. It's about—" James lowered his voice even more, too low for Mindy to understand.

She opened her eyes to narrow slits. The two men had their heads together. She could hear the hiss of James's whisper, but couldn't understand a thing.

The big man nodded. "I'll get the knife."

"Leave it. It'll make him think he's smarter than us." James coughed again and took a deep breath. "Let's get out of here."

He opened the door on the north wall, and the two men disappeared through it.

Blinded by the bright light from the open door, Mindy scooted blindly across the dirt floor toward Deke. Several times, her bottom bumped against the raised metal rails.

As her night vision came back and she made out his silhouette, she noticed the blacker-than-black pool that was spreading under him. It wasn't just a trick of the shadows.

It was blood.

Deke's blood. That's why he'd kept slipping as he'd fought James. She'd seen James jerk Deke's knife out of his side with a roar and brandish it as Deke dove for the gun.

The lantern's light had reflected off the blade as it sliced an arc through the air. Behind the blade, red droplets had scattered in a fine spray that caught the light like tiny rubies.

Then Deke had gone down.

"Deke," she whispered, touching his forehead with her fingertips. She knew it would be foolish to assume that their kidnappers were gone for good. So she kept an eye out for the least hint of light.

"Deke, wake up. Are you okay?"

He groaned and stirred.

"Deke? Answer me."

He made a low growling noise in his throat and tried to push himself to his hands and knees, but his right arm wouldn't hold his weight. He collapsed again.

She didn't know what to do. Watching him struggle helplessly sent fear burrowing into her—soul-deep fear. She'd never seen him weak or injured. The sight was like a slap to her face.

Deke Cunningham was flesh and bone, just like everyone else. Just like her. He was breakable.

She pressed her palm against his forehead. "Wake up," she pleaded. "I'm going to need your help. I don't think I can stand up by myself."

He made a noise. It could have been a groan or a brief snort of laughter. Carefully, holding his right arm against his side, he rolled up into a sitting position, got his legs under him, and pushed himself to his feet.

Mindy looked up. His face, distorted by the wavering lantern light, was a grimacing mask of pain. She had no idea what being Tasered felt like, but if it could do this to her ex-husband, it had to be bad.

But what really worried her was the knife wound in his arm.

In typical Deke fashion, he composed his face, then looked down at her and crooked his mouth into a half smile. He held out his hand.

"You can't just give me a hand up," she said wryly. "I'm way beyond that. This is not going to be pretty." She rolled over to all-fours, and slowly, using the wall for support, she carefully pushed herself to her knees.

"Can you come around and get your left hand under my arm and lift?" She was embarrassed by her helplessness in front of him, and he picked up on that.

"What's the matter, Min? I've seen you in more interesting positions than this." He moved to her right side and hooked his elbow under her arm.

"This is different."

He lifted her with a grunt. "Yeah. You weigh more."

"Not funny," she grunted, as she managed to stand with a whole lot of help from him. "I'm sorry. I know that hurt you."

"No problem," he muttered.

She stepped to one side so the lantern light shone fully on him, and gasped when she saw the amount of blood that soaked the arm of his jacket.

"Oh, no, Deke. All that blood."

"It's okay," he muttered. "What about you? Did that bastard hurt you?"

She shook her head. "You took care of me. Now I need to take care of you. Take off your jacket."

Once he'd managed to peel the jacket off, she lifted the slashed cotton fabric away from the wound and hissed through her teeth.

"It's nothing," Deke protested, pulling back.

"Oh, no, trust me. It's *something*," she retorted. "You've got at least a six-inch gash. You need stitches."

"How do you suggest I get 'em?"

She winced at his gruff tone. He didn't like to show weakness—any kind of weakness. Not physical, and certainly not emotional. He never had. He'd learned early that weakness drew predators like a shark to blood. So he'd long ago decided that the best defense was an impenetrable shield and a strong offense.

Over the years she'd watched him learn those lessons, from his alcoholic father, from the other kids in school, from life. She'd been there for every brick he'd laid to fortify his heart.

She understood that his anger wasn't aimed at her. She just happened to be in the way. Just as she'd been many times before.

With the ease of long practice, she ignored his words and his attitude. "I can't sew up the wound, but I can wrap it."

"Min, we don't have time—"

"Just shut up and take off your shirt."

With a frustrated sigh, he complied. He kept his right arm still as he undid the buttons with his left hand. When his shirt was hanging open over his bare chest, she took his left hand. "I'll get this button," she murmured.

He let her undo the sleeve, then he shrugged the shirt off with a groan, and carefully slid it down his right arm.

"Oh, Deke. Look what he did to you." Dark bruises covered his side, where James had kicked him with those silver-toed boots. His right forearm was coated with blood, and in taking off his shirt he'd smeared the blood all over his abdomen and chest.

He shrugged, sending ripples along the muscles of his shoulders and arms.

Mindy couldn't take her eyes off him. They'd been married for nine years and lovers for two years before that. She knew every inch of his body. Every curve of muscle. Every scar.

He seemed leaner, harder, and yet at the same time less harsh. Every bit as handsome, though. And every bit as sexy.

Memories washed over her—the feel of his hot, naked body against hers. That silk-over-steel strength and the unimaginable thrill of being filled by him.

As she'd told him many times, their problem was never the sex. She was just as turned on by him as she'd always been. Maybe more.

She still wanted him. She was eight months pregnant, cold, hungry and terrified, and yet the desire was still there, humming, vibrating, singing, inside her.

Stop it. The stirrings she felt were just hormones. Hormones and habit.

Even as she lectured herself, she knew she was lying. Deke's golden-tanned skin, his sleekly defined muscles, the slope of his broad shoulders and the harshly beautiful planes of his abs, hips and flanks, were as familiar to her as her own body.

Actually, more familiar right now. Considering that for the past eight months her body had been in a constant state of change and still was.

She rubbed her tummy where his son was wiggling around. Her little Sprout was proof of that. Even on the day she'd buried her mother, the one thing that had succeeded in drawing her out of the poignant sadness was Deke, with the sweet gentleness that he revealed only to her.

Dear heavens, she loved him.

No, I don't, her rational brain responded immediately.

But arguing with herself was useless. She might not be able to live with him. But she would always love him.

"Well?" he grumbled. "Are you just going to stand there while I bleed to death?"

His voice sounded irritated, but his eyes held a spark of amusement, and his mouth a ghost of a smirk.

Her face burned with embarrassment. Damn him, he knew what she was thinking. *Great.* Something else that hadn't changed. A splinter of irritation stung away some of her desire.

"Sorry," she muttered. She yanked the shirt out of his hands and ripped it into strips.

"Min, I didn't mean—"

"I need something to wash out the wound." She spoke briskly, not giving him time to apologize. She glanced around, her gaze stopping on the lantern. "The oil."

"No. No way."

"Why not? It's hot, and it's a good disinfectant."

Deke shook his head. "It's a better fuel source. As soon as you're done playing nurse I'm putting that sucker out and taking it with us. We'll need it."

"I don't want to wrap your arm without washing it."

"Wash it later. Wrap it now. That sonofoabitch is going to come back, once he licks his wounds. I don't plan for us to be here."

"Did you hear James and the other man talking?" she asked as she quickly and efficiently wrapped his arm, doing her best to keep the edges of the wound together without tying the bandage too tight.

"Talking? When?"

"After he Tasered you."

"Seems like I heard something, but it didn't make sense. It's hard to think when electricity's frying your brain. I think I passed out for a few seconds." He rubbed his temple with his left hand. "Why?"

"They had a perfectly good chance to capture us both again. You were paralyzed by the Taser and I was on the ground, helpless. But James told the other guy not to. He said 'it's not about capturing them.' Then he said to leave you the knife. He said, It'll 'make him think he's smarter.'" She looked up. "What's going on?"

Deke shook his head. "He's playing cat and mouse with me. He wants me to believe I can get us out of here."

"*I* believe you can."

He gave her a ghost of a smile. "Thanks. But I have

a feeling I'm a little outnumbered. I'm pretty sure there are more than two of them. I'd bet money that every exit is guarded."

"So—we're mice in a maze? And if we run the maze correctly our reward is death?"

"Something like that."

Those three flat words frightened her more than his anger or even his fear ever could. He was the bravest man she'd ever known. So why was he accepting the inevitable now, after all the things he'd endured?

Endured. That was it! He knew they were outnumbered and outflanked. His only choice, given the handicap of having to worry about her, was to conserve his strength and hers—to outwait and outwit the enemy.

Something he'd said earlier, when he was trying to stop James from shooting her in the head, niggled at the edge of her brain. But she'd been so scared that her brain had been incapable of processing what he said. She tried to replay his words in her head, but they flitted away, leaving her with nothing but a question.

"Who is the enemy?"

"What?"

She jumped. "What?"

"You said something."

"No, I didn't." Had she spoken aloud? She savagely ripped the ends of her makeshift bandage, berating herself for not watching what she said.

"Ouch. Where's the knife? Cutting the fabric would be easier—and less painful than tearing it."

"It fell over there." She gestured in the direction of the door."

"Hurry up. I need to get it. And by the way, yes, you did say something. You said, 'who's the enemy?'"

She tied the torn ends of the bandage to keep it in place.

"Did I? Well, it's a good question. You never did tell me what you did that made Frank James kidnap me, and why he's playing cat and mouse with you. He obviously knows who you are."

He looked at his fingers and flexed them, as if the most important thing in the world to him was making sure the bandage wasn't too tight.

"Deke, look at me. Who's behind all this?"

His head ducked a fraction lower, then he raised his gaze to hers. "I've never seen Frank James before."

Mindy studied his face. This was her childhood sweetheart, her lover, her former husband. The man she knew better than anyone in the world. The set of his jaw, the tiny wrinkles at the corners of his eyes, the flat line of his mouth, told her he was holding something back.

She almost laughed. *So what's new?*

He swiveled and headed toward the wooden door.

"Deke, what are you—?"

Then he held up the lighter and kicked around in the dirt. He was looking for his knife.

She watched him and tried to remember what he'd said back there when Frank James was holding her with a gun to her head. He'd tried to bluff James out of pulling the trigger by distracting him with insults and playing on his obvious cowardice.

He'd said something that hadn't fit with the rest of his verbal jabs. Something that sounded real—and disturbing. She could almost hear it in her brain. Almost, but not quite.

Suddenly, the memory hit her. His voice echoed in her head.

You couldn't pull this off alone. You're working for Novus Ordo.

Novus Ordo. "Oh, dear heavens," she choked out through the hand that had flown to her mouth. The realization stole her breath. The man who'd captured and tortured Deke. "It's Novus Ordo."

"What?" He looked at her suspiciously.

"Don't even try that 'I don't know what you're talking about' innocent tone with me, Deke Cunningham." She took a step backward, as if distance could protect her from the knowledge that was swirling around in her brain.

After Deke had come back from Mahjidastan, he'd been a different man. He'd never told her what had happened to him over there, but his best friend had.

Rook had told her how Novus Ordo, the infamous terrorist, had captured Deke when his helicopter went down. He'd described some of the torture Deke had endured at his hands.

Rook had begged her to stick with him, to help him heal.

And she'd tried. But Deke had refused her help—or anyone else's. Refused vehemently. Then he'd gone away and left her alone.

The empty shell of his body had still been there, but the man she'd loved all her life had disappeared—into drink, into depression, into self-loathing. The man she'd believed was unbreakable had been broken.

So in self-defense, before he sucked her into the abyss with him, she'd filed for divorce.

Then Rook had been assassinated, and the speculation had started—on a national scale. Novus Ordo, the most feared terrorist since Bin Laden, was rumored to have ordered the death of the highly decorated former Air Force colonel Robert Kenneth Castle because of a personal grievance.

Mindy had feared that Rook's death would send Deke over the edge, but through Irina she knew that he had moved to Castle Ranch and had taken over BHSAR operations, while Irina handled the business aspects and searched for proof that Rook was still alive.

It seemed that Rook's death had brought Deke back to life.

"That terrorist is behind this, isn't he?"

"Come on, Mindy."

Mindy lifted her chin pugnaciously. "No. You come on. Don't treat me like an idiot. Irina stops searching for Rook and a week later here we are, being held captive because you know something that you're not telling me. I heard what you said to Frank James. I can put the pieces together. Novus Ordo thinks you know where Rook is, doesn't he?"

Deke's eyes narrowed and the tiny wrinkles between his brows deepened. He scowled at her.

"Oh my God, you do!"

For an instant, Deke stared at her as if she were a ghost. Then his mouth and jaw relaxed. He shook his head. "No. I don't know where he is."

Mindy frowned at him. "Why are you—?" One look in his eyes and her question died on her lips. Without moving his head, he shifted his gaze above her, then to his right and his left then back to stare at her.

She understood immediately. He suspected that they were being watched or listened to. She gave him a small nod and took a deep breath.

"You really don't know?" she asked, doing her best

to sound like she believed what she was saying. "But what about all those rumors that he's still alive?"

"They've stuck around because Irina wouldn't give up. But now she has. Rook Castle is dead."

"So what about Frank James? Do you think he's working for Novus?"

"He could be. I'd have thought Novus was smarter than that, but maybe not. He may have ordered Rook assassinated, but the body was never recovered. If I were Novus, and I thought my nemesis was still alive, I'd probably panic if his wife suddenly quit searching for him." He made an impatient sound. "Are you done playing nurse yet?"

She gave the bandage on his forearm a final inspection. "Fine. I'm done. But if it doesn't stop bleeding. I'll have to put spiderwebs on it."

"Hell, no, you won't." Deke stared at her. "What are you talking about—spiderwebs?"

"They can promote clotting. They work by—"

"Min." Deke held up his hand. "I don't care how they work. I won't bleed anymore."

She shot him an ironic glance. "You'll control it with your steely resolve?"

He nodded. "Damn straight I will."

Mindy chuckled. "That's my hero."

Deke winced at her words. She'd said them unintentionally, he was sure. She'd called him her hero ever since high school. Ever since the first time they'd made love, when she was seventeen.

He'd been careful and slow, determined to show her what sex was all about. Afterward, she'd lain in his arms, panting and spent, and awed by what had happened to her.

Eventually, she'd turned toward him. She'd touched his cheek and murmured, "You're my hero, and I will always love you."

He blinked and shook his head slightly, pushing the memories back—way back—to the place where he kept them locked up. That was a long time ago, when she'd loved him.

He was no hero now. *Hah.* Never had been. He'd never brought her anything but heartbreak. No wonder she hadn't wanted him to know about her baby. She'd tried to protect herself and her child from more pain.

And what had he done? He'd left her alone and vulnerable against attack. He was the one who'd gotten her into this, and now he had to get her out.

Without a scratch.

"Let's get out of here. I'm sure James already knows where we'll end up. But hell, there's nothing I can do about that." He carefully shrugged into his shearling jacket and grabbed the oil lantern off the nail.

The first thing he did was examine the slatted wooden door on the north wall. There was no knob, just a keyhole. "This is where they disappeared?"

Mindy nodded.

He pushed against it, but it didn't budge. Then he transferred the lantern to his right hand and tried to get a grip on it by inserting his fingers into the slats. "It's locked."

"What did you find in the other direction?" Mindy asked.

"Pretty much what I expected. I'm guessing this hotel was built here so they could use this tunnel junction as its basement." He pointed toward the south tunnel. "No coal car rails in that tunnel. So I'm thinking it's either closed or it's a dead end. I didn't go very far. I didn't want to leave you." He grimaced. "I left you too long as it was."

"You didn't know—"

"I should have." He gestured at the floor. Unlike the south tunnel, this branch had two sets of rails on its dirt-and-rock-covered floor. They extended down the corridor as far as he could see. "See? These rails have been used. You can see where they're worn. Obviously this tunnel has seen a lot of people come through it."

"But why would they need rails here? This looks like the end of the line—or the beginning."

"Look at that." He pointed at the planks and boards surrounding the trapdoor where he'd crawled in. "That was a door into the hotel basement. This other door may be to the mine foreman's office, or some other administrative type. They probably used a man car to travel from here down into the belly of the mine."

"Man car?"

"Traveled on the rails like the coal cars, but held passengers—the miners, of course—to carry them down to the deeper parts of the mine. But the inspectors, the bosses, the foreman, would travel down there, too."

"How do you know all this?"

Deke sent her a wry smile. "I read up on it as soon as I figured out where your phone call came from."

He bent over and picked up his knife, and then pointed to the trapdoor that led into the hotel basement.

"Can't go that way," he said, conjuring up a picture of Mindy getting on hands and knees to crawl through to the hotel's basement.

Not happening.

He pressed his bandaged arm against his side and

clenched his teeth against the stinging pain as he looked at the two tunnels. His instincts had always been excellent. They'd gotten him out of dangerous situations many times.

But right now he had no idea which tunnel to take. What would Novus expect him to do? Take the south tunnel, which appeared to be abandoned and might lead to a dead end, trapping them? Or follow the coal-car rails, which careered down a steep incline to a tippling station, where they'd dump the coal into the larger railroad cars?

He cursed under his breath.

"What is it?" Mindy asked. "What's wrong?"

He pointed to one of the tunnels. "What do you think, Min? The lady? Or the tiger?"

Chapter Six

"I don't think I can go any farther," Mindy said. She hated to tell Deke that. Hated to let him down. Her fingers were cramping from holding on to his belt and trying to stay directly behind him.

He'd been guiding her in the darkness, warning her of rough patches or a curve. They were walking on a steep downward incline—going deeper underground.

When he'd chosen the abandoned south tunnel over the north one that appeared to be open, she'd been surprised. But she'd kept her mouth shut, trusting him.

Twice already, he'd stumbled over broken boards and piles of dirt and rocks. Once he'd hit his head on a sagging roof beam.

She'd never been afraid of the dark until now.

This darkness was *total.* The sensation was claustrophobic, dizzying, terrifying. She couldn't see anything, not even her own hand. Even holding on to Deke's belt, she found herself drifting off to the right or left. And sometimes she felt like she was leaning—not standing up straight.

When that happened, she'd suddenly jerk upright. That earned her a bout of vertigo.

The vertigo would trigger panic, which would disturb Sprout, and that increased her nervousness. Especially when she thought about how deep underground they were.

Not even having Deke with her helped.

"Hang in there a little longer, Min." His voice sounded strained.

If Deke was worried, then it was seriously time to panic. "Deke—I can't!"

"Just a little more, Min. I think I hear something."

Her heart pounded. "What?"

He reached behind him and touched her hand. "Water running. Listen."

He stopped, and she stepped up closer to him. "I don't hear anything."

"I've got specially trained ears."

She heard the smile in his voice. And appreciated it. He was trying to keep it light. For her. Trying to help her through the blackness.

She sucked in a deep breath that hitched at the top like a sob. "You do—have nice ears."

"Nice? They're superb." He gently extricated her fingers from his belt and pulled her close, wrapping his strong arm around her waist.

"Listen," he whispered in her ear.

She started to tell him that as long as he was breathing that close to her ear, it didn't matter what was out there. She wouldn't be able to hear Niagara Falls.

As if she'd spoken aloud, he held his breath. She held hers, too.

And heard a faint ripple.

"There it is," she whispered in awe.

"Told you." His arm tightened around her waist. For

the first time he seemed, if not comfortable, at least not especially uncomfortable with her rounded, unfamiliar shape.

Then, to her surprise, his head dipped and he nuzzled her hair.

"Let's go find that water," he said, straightening. "If we're real lucky, there will be another lantern there. Or some torches."

"Can you—" Mindy paused and took a breath. "I'm sorry, Deke, but can you light the lantern?"

"As soon as we get to the water, okay? I don't want to waste the oil."

Mindy felt like crying. She was so tired, so hungry, and so afraid that she'd never see light again. Her skin was clammy and cold. The air had been growing a little warmer as they went deeper, but suddenly, her neck felt cool—cooler than normal. She shivered as Deke took her hand and tucked it into his belt at the small of his back.

"Deke? I think I feel something."

Deke froze in midstride. "Something with the baby? Are you okay?"

"No. I mean, yes. I'm fine. It's not the baby. It's like air. I feel air on my neck."

He stayed still. Yet she knew from the change in the tension of his back muscles and from her familiarity with his body that he had his hand up and was testing the air.

"Come on," he said, and moved forward.

As they got closer to the running water and the sound increased, Mindy started thinking she saw something. Which was impossible, since there was no light anywhere.

She blinked, making sure her eyes were open.

Sure enough, there was something not quite hellhole-black in front of her. All at once she got her balance back, and the vertigo went anyway.

"Deke, do you—?"

"Shh!" His hand reached back and connected with her tummy. She felt him flinch, but he didn't jerk away. "I need to check this out," he whispered. "Stay here."

Terror gripped her, causing her little Sprout to stir restlessly. She grabbed Deke's hand and squeezed it. "Deke, please. Don't leave me. Not in the dark."

"Stay here!" Deke's voice brooked no argument.

Mindy stayed. She trembled and hugged her tummy. Her eyes devoured the faint hint of less-than-total blackness in front of her. Her ears strained to hear the smallest sound that would tell her that Deke was all right. And her pulse drummed so hard and fast that she thought she might pass out. But she stayed.

Suddenly, a shadow moved directly in her line of sight. At first she wasn't sure she saw it. She attributed it to the darkness and her fear and anticipation. But it kept coming closer.

Looming, menacing, like a spectre out of a dark lagoon, it stalked toward her.

Her pounding heart sped up even more, until she could feel the throbbing in her temples, in her wrists, even in the restless movements of her baby inside her. Then Sprout kicked her—hard.

She gasped.

"Mindy?"

Deke. His precious voice was right there. In front of her. It was Deke.

"Deke?" she breathed.

"Yeah. I was counting my footsteps. I didn't mean to scare you."

"What did you find?"

His hand touched her upper arm and slid down until he found her fingers. He clutched them.

"Wait and see." He couldn't disguise the excitement in his voice.

Mindy's pounding heart calmed down immediately. Right now, here in this menacing, dark place, she caught a glimpse of the handsome, cocky teenager she'd fallen in love with so many years ago.

He'd been supremely arrogant—certain that there was no obstacle he couldn't conquer, no mountain he couldn't climb. Happy and teasing and gentle, excited to show her a new discovery. From the moment she first laid eyes on him, he'd been her hero.

She hadn't seen him in eight long months, although she'd come close to calling him a dozen times to tell him he was going to be a father. Then she'd thought better of it, decided that she and her child would be better off if she never got sucked into his self-destructive life.

Seeing him now, she wasn't sure she'd made the right decision.

She squeezed his fingers back. "Take me." She heard the tremor in her voice.

He put his arm around her waist and led her forward and around a curve. As soon as they rounded the corner, Mindy saw a silvery-blue light shining down from above like a spotlight. In the light's circle was the spring they'd heard. It warbled and bubbled, its shimmering water reflecting the light like something magical as it flowed over pale rocks.

"Oh—" She was speechless.

Deke's hand tightened on her waist and he nuzzled the delicate skin right in front of her ear. "Welcome to your fantasy forest glen, my lady," he whispered, a smile in his voice.

"This is so beautiful. How—?"

She felt him shrug. "Best I can figure, this is a major artery of the old mine. They put it here, where the underground spring carved out this natural cavern." He started forward, guiding her at his side as he talked.

"The light comes from what looks like a wooden chimney way above us. Look." He pulled her close to the stream and pointed above their heads.

Almost too distracted by the sheer incredible relief of seeing light before her eyes, Mindy finally assimilated what he'd said and looked upward.

"I think it's a ventilation shaft. They sometimes had problems with the air quality in these mines. So they'd build shafts to let in fresh air."

"And light!" she exclaimed.

Deke's finger touched her chin and his thumb urged her to raise her head.

She did. When she met his dark gaze lit by blue fire, her knees grew weak.

"And light," he murmured. Then he bent his head and kissed her.

His kiss was like coming home. Like heaven. Like life. She melted into the warmth and sensuality of his mouth on hers, and responded. He kissed her more intimately, and a thrill slid though her entire body, settling in her sexual core.

Then Sprout kicked her. She drew in a small, sharp breath and instinctively pressed her palms against her side.

Deke backed away instantly. "What was that?" he asked. "Are you all right?"

Mindy smiled sadly. "It's our son kicking. He likes to get me right here, in the side."

"Our—" Deke looked down at her tummy, then back up. His eyes glittered in the pale blue light that barely managed to chase the shadows away from the circle under the ventilation shaft.

"Our son," he whispered, an expression of awe lighting his face.

His words, his voice cut through to her heart. She heard fear, but along with the fear was a note of wonder.

And there he was—the man she'd never seen, the man she'd always known he could be. If he'd ever learn to trust her, or himself, enough.

She nodded and lifted her hand to touch his cheek.

But he took another step back, straightened and turned away. He walked over to the edge of the stream.

"You need some water," he stated matter-of-factly without turning around. "I found an old candle bucket in the corner. I cleaned it with sand and anchored it between some rocks so the flowing water would rinse it out."

Mindy felt like he'd ripped her heart right out of her chest. She'd always wondered what it would take to break through the wall he raised whenever someone got too close. Her love had never been enough. She'd hoped little Sprout would be.

But his damn pride and fear had overpowered him.

So he'd forced his feelings—what he considered his weakness—back behind the wall that shielded his heart.

He kneeled and picked up the bucket and brought it to her, half-filled with water. His face was expressionless, his voice remote. "Here. I'll hold it while you drink."

She held the sides of the bucket between her palms and guided it to her lips. The galvanized metal rim was icy-cold, and she had trouble swallowing the water past the lump in her throat, but the few swallows she managed to get down tasted heavenly.

It was sweet and cold and thoroughly refreshing. It ran over the edge of the bucket and dripped down her chin onto her breasts and tummy.

Deke held the bucket patiently. As soon as she'd finished drinking, he turned on his heel and with his back to her, he drank his fill.

"Come over here," he said without turning around.

As she followed him over to the wall, she took in what was around her. There was a small stack of railroad-ties against the wall that was obviously intended as a crude bench. Buckets were scattered around, sitting up or overturned. On the ground to the side of the railroad tie bench sat a large metal tray covered with a piece of steel screen. Several feet beyond the bench stood an old vehicle that looked like a wagon with a cover over it.

"What is all this?" she asked Deke.

"I think this was probably a popular lunch spot with the coal miners. Somebody took the trouble to build the bench and the stove. And check that out." He pointed to the vehicle.

"That's a man car. Covered with a blanket. Look at

the lanterns attached to the sides. They look like they still have oil in them."

Mindy turned her head to look, but she must have moved too fast, because dizziness overwhelmed her.

Deke caught her arm. "Whoa. Sit down over here. You're exhausted, and I am *not* about to try and get you back on your feet if you faint."

She made a face at him as he tugged on her arm until she followed him over to the bench. He gently pushed her down.

"Now stay there. The miners who worked down here had a pretty clever setup. We'll have some dinner in a few minutes."

"Dinner?" she said weakly. As if on cue, her stomach growled and Sprout wiggled and pounded against her side.

"Yeah. Do you see the silver flashes in the stream?"

"No." She squinted. "Maybe."

"They're fish."

"Fish? There are fish down here?"

"I haven't figured out what kind they are, but I'm about to."

"What are you going to do?"

He picked up one of the buckets and brought it over for her to see. "Somebody punched holes in the bottom of this bucket."

"A lot of holes," Mindy agreed.

"I'm thinking they used it to fish—like a net. With any luck, I can anchor it in the water and come up with a few fish."

"Fish," Mindy breathed. "I'm so hungry I could manage to eat them raw. But—?"

Deke grinned at her and pointed at the pile of ashes and twigs. "Don't worry. We'll cook them the old-fashioned way."

WITHIN TWENTY MINUTES, Deke had a bucketful of fish, and the legs of his jeans were soaked through. He climbed out of the stream, shivering when his bare feet hit the air. The spring was quite a few degrees colder than the surrounding atmosphere.

He brought the dripping bucket over to the campfire site and set it on a piece of railroad tie.

Raising his head, he started to speak to Mindy, but her eyes were closed and her lips were barely parted. She was asleep.

Compressing his mouth into a thin line, Deke sat on his haunches and watched her for a few minutes. Her soft mouth, her delicate brows and the eyelashes that lay on her cheeks like big fuzzy caterpillars, all the little parts of her that were tattooed on his heart.

His gaze slid down her neck and breasts to her tummy. Pregnant, she looked and acted so different. She had a contentment about her that she'd never had when they were together.

Just the sight of her soft, serene expression made his heart hurt. Why was she serene and happy now? Was it because he was out of her life? Why hadn't he been able to bring that look to her face?

As soon as the question rose in his mind, he knew the answer. It was simple. He could never give her ease and contentment, because he was a breaker. He broke promises, broke vows, broke hearts.

He sighed. Even if he couldn't give her contentment, he could give her his protection. He owed her that much. He'd brought her into this mess.

He resolved to let her sleep until he got the fish cooked, then once she ate, he'd make sure she slept some more.

For several minutes, he explored the cavern. It wasn't huge, but it was like a vast, empty auditorium compared to the dark, narrow tunnels that fed into and out of it.

The main tunnel had eight sets of rails that ran downhill, parallel to the stream. Four of the sets came from the tunnel behind him. Its incline wasn't nearly as steep as the north one. The other four came from the east—the tunnel from the anteroom in the hotel basement—and joined the first four just above the sharp downhill incline.

He continued northward, examining the walls for other tunnels. In a pocket close to the rail intersection, he found a pile of branches and twigs. Beside the pile was a bucket of kindling and one about half-filled with candles.

Deke propped his fists on his hips and looked back toward the ventilation shaft, thinking about luck and coincidence.

A cozy campsite with readily available fuel, a water source and a light source. *It was too good to be true.* It could easily be the latest in a series of traps set by Novus Ordo. Force them to take this tunnel, bring them to a veritable underground paradise complete with everything they needed to fill their stomachs and calm their minds. Then attack them while they were asleep.

He had to hand it to Novus. It was amazing what he'd managed to put together on a moment's notice. Amazing and frightening. Deke wondered how many men Novus had in the U.S. who were available and willing to drop everything on an hour's notice to carry out a focused and unrelenting attack.

Oddly enough, he no longer felt that prickle on the back of his neck. Maybe Novus's men hadn't managed to wire this section of the mine.

He thought about what Frank James had said to him.

You'll be hungry and thirsty and tired. Your gal there'll be pretty darn sick from hunger and exhaustion.

It made perfect sense, knowing Novus. He was wearing Deke down, as he'd done before. After his capture in Mahjidastan, Deke had been trussed so tightly his shoulders had been dislocated, then he'd been thrown into a filthy, stinking tent. Each day at the same time, a robed man brought him a bowl of foul-tasting mush and one of dirty water. Then hours later, another robed and masked man would come in, order Deke to rise to his knees, spin the cylinder of a revolver, and fire it at Deke's head.

Those two visits took about six to eight minutes out of his day. The other twenty-three hours and fifty-odd minutes, he was left alone to think about the next day, when they would come again.

Deke pushed his fingers through his hair and rubbed the back of his neck as a deep shudder racked him. He wanted to give Novus and his ridiculous toy cowboy something to think about. He wanted to leave this lovely, compelling little cavern behind and spend the night poised for ambush, waiting for them to come looking for him.

But Mindy was already dog-tired; her face was drawn and pale. Right now, the most important thing was to make sure she got nourishment and rest. For herself and her baby.

He brought a pile of branches back to the campfire

and, using a candle stub for a starter, soon got a nice fire going. He washed a small piece of screening to put the filleted fish on, then set it on the stove to cook.

By the time the fish were cooked, Mindy was stirring. Deke took the makeshift plate over and set it beside her on the railroad-tie bench.

"What's this?" she murmured sleepily.

"Dinner. Unfortunately, this is the entire menu. I don't even have any salt—or utensils."

"This is perfect."

The fish was tender and fell apart easily. Deke held back and let Mindy have as much as she wanted. She downed at least six of the small filets. When she sat back and sighed with contentment, Deke, who had been busying himself with the fire, finished them off.

Then he brought her a bucket of water. "Drink first," he said, "then wash up."

She obeyed, then glared at him. "Now, you bring some fresh water up here and some sand or gravel."

He frowned at her.

"I'm going to wash your arm. *And* I want some of that lantern oil to disinfect it."

"I told you, Min—"

"I don't care!" She held up a hand. "You said yourself the lanterns on that car had oil in them. Now bring me some. And get those bandages off and use the bucket with the holes in it to wash them in the stream."

It was Deke's turn to obey. By the time she'd scrubbed the gash in his arm with sand and water, and poured lantern oil into it—which burned like a sonofabitch—he was cold and strangely tired.

"Long before we had modern ways of cleaning and

disinfecting wounds, people used kerosene, gasoline, even gunpowder, to clean wounds."

Deke uttered a short laugh. "I guess I'm lucky we don't have a gun. I can hear you now, telling me that fire is the best disinfectant."

"Don't make fun. If it gets any worse, I may have to burn it. See the inflamed areas at the edges of the wound?" she asked.

Deke didn't want to look. He felt like his arm was on fire, and yet the rest of him was shivering with cold.

"That's cellulitis. It means your wound is infected. I'll bet you have fever. Damn it, Deke. If you'd let me clean it when I wanted to, this wouldn't have happened."

"It's not a problem."

"Yes, it is. I've got to keep an eye on this. If we see red streaks starting up your arm, that'll mean the infection is serious."

"I'll be fine."

"You're already not fine. Now bring me those bandages."

It took only a few minutes for Mindy to wrap his arm. Afterward, he quickly cleaned up the campsite, doing his best to make it look as if it hadn't been disturbed. Then he helped Mindy cross the shallow spring.

During his exploration earlier, he'd found a pocketlike alcove in the wall on that side of the spring. It was deep enough that they could sit in the shadows and see into the tunnels without exposing themselves.

"I'm going to have to sit you on the ground," he told Mindy. "But I promise there aren't any bugs."

She chuckled quietly. "Don't worry. Bugs are the least of my worries right now."

Deke looked at her, wondering how he was going to get her to the ground. If it weren't for his arm, he'd pick her up and lay her down, but she was right about his wound. It seemed to be getting hotter and more tender. He shivered.

If her efforts didn't stop the infection, he was terribly afraid he might not make it much further under his own steam.

But he didn't tell her that.

"How do you want to do this?" he asked.

"If you can hold my hands, I can lower myself to the ground. Getting up will be a different story, though."

He helped her to the ground. "Are you cold?"

She shook her head. "Not too bad. It's a lot warmer over here than on the other side of the creek. Wonder why?"

"There could be a fire smoldering on the other side of this wall. I don't smell anything, so I'm not sure."

"A fire?"

"Sometimes the coal in these underground passages catches fire. They can burn slowly for years before anything happens." He put his hand on the dirt wall behind them. The wall did feel several degrees warmer than the wall on the other side.

"Years? And what kind of anything?"

"Yep, years. Like fifty or so in some cases. Eventually the fire will use up all the air in the mine and can burst through the surface."

Mindy turned her head to stare at him. "It won't happen today, will it?"

He couldn't help but smile. "Not if we're lucky."

"Why couldn't you have just said 'Who knows?' when I asked you why the wall was warm."

"Ask me again."

She laughed quietly and Deke felt her shoulders move. He lifted his left arm and slid it around her.

"Why don't you try to sleep," he said. "I'll keep an eye out for predators."

Mindy's shoulders stiffened. "Predators? You mean Frank James? Or are there bears and things around?"

He tightened his arm around her and bent to whisper in her ear. "You let me worry about bears and things. You just worry about getting some sleep. You're exhausted, and you've got to rest so your baby can rest."

"*Your* baby," she murmured.

The two words ripped through him like a bullet.

His baby.

He still couldn't make those two words work together. *He* didn't have a baby. He couldn't.

Not with his legacy. Not if he was anything at all like his father. *If?* Hell. There was no if about it. He *was* like his father.

His dad had been a mean, abusive drunk. Deke knew that his own battle had taken a different turn. He'd drunk a lot and tried drugs a little. But early on he'd discovered that he was a surly drunk rather than a violent one, like good old Dad. He didn't lash out physically, but he definitely lashed out verbally, with hurtful, cutting jabs at anybody who happened to be in his way.

No. Fatherhood was not for him. No innocent child should ever be subjected to what he could dish out when he was under the influence. A very good reason why he never drank anymore. Not even beer.

"Deke?"

His thoughts slammed back into the present, and he

realized he was squeezing Mindy's shoulders. He relaxed his hand. "Yeah, sugar?"

"You don't have to be afraid of him."

The image of his father, eyes black as night and deep lines in his scowling face, rose before his vision for a few seconds before he realized she was referring to the baby.

"This little Sprout is a lot like you already. And he's only just getting ready to be born."

"Sprout?"

She laughed. "I call him that. It just came out one day when I was talking to him." She rubbed her tummy with both hands. "Do you want to feel him move? It seems like he moves almost all the time now. I don't know when he sleeps."

"I, uh—"

"Come on. Give me your hands."

Mindy took his hands and placed them on her rounded tummy, which was much firmer than he'd expected it to be. He'd always figured a pregnant tummy would be sort of springy and mushy. But hers felt like a basketball, round and hard.

"Is that how it's supposed to be? All hard like that?"

Mindy laughed, and her laugh slid through him like old times.

Then something moved. Deke jerked his hands away.

"Okay, you big scaredy-cat, it's just your son."

Just?

She pressed his hands down again and slid them over to her side. "Here. Here's his foot. *Mmh.* Feel that? He just kicked me. It's his favorite pastime."

"He kicked," Deke whispered in awe. "That was his foot."

"See? You can tell he's very healthy. He's pretty big, too. The doctor thinks he'll probably weigh at least seven pounds."

"Seven pounds."

Mindy inclined her head and gently bumped Deke's chin. "You're funny. All you're doing is repeating what I say. Is Sprout here that intimidating?"

Slowly, he nodded.

Mindy yawned, so he extracted his hands from hers and put his arm around her again. "Lean against me and sleep. I'll keep watch."

Mindy tucked her head under his chin and settled against him, with her tummy pressed against his side. "Then you have to wake me up to stand guard while *you* sleep."

Deke settled gently back against the warm wall and watched the tunnel in front of them, wondering how long it would take for Frank James to find them.

Chapter Seven

He drove the SUV along the fence line, using only the moon's light to examine the chain links for tears or breaks. Headlights would ruin his night vision. Besides, although everyone knew it was his shift to guard the remote perimeter of Castle Ranch, at least without headlights they couldn't see exactly where he was or what he was doing.

Everyone at the ranch was getting cabin fever, so Matt Parker had suggested that the specialists patrol the perimeter. All of them had jumped at the idea. It wasn't their nature to sit idle while one of their own was in trouble.

He drove over a ridge—and there it was. Exactly what he'd been looking for. On a spread the size of Castle Ranch, there had to be sections that were totally hidden. And this one was perfect for his purposes. The top of the ridge had a clear view of the front of the ranch. Its other side was completely hidden from all directions by scrub brush. A sniper could hide out here for hours—days, if necessary.

His hands shook on the steering wheel. At least, the vengeance he'd longed for all these years was within his reach.

MINDY SLEPT LIGHTLY. It had been weeks since she'd slept well, thanks to her little Sprout. Now her bed consisted of hard-packed dirt in an underground cave in early April. Which meant the nights were still quite cold. If she didn't have Deke to lean on and snuggle up against, she'd be half or maybe three-quarters frozen by now.

But she did have Deke. At some time while she was asleep, he'd managed to maneuver so that her head was on his chest and her tummy rested in the cradle created by his thighs.

She closed her eyes and relaxed against him. Her right ear was pressed to his chest and his strong, steady heartbeat set a rhythm for hers.

And her Sprout's. She could feel the baby. He felt like he was gently rocking himself to the comforting drumbeat of Deke's heart.

The spring provided a lilting melody to the bass beat of Deke's heart, and water dripping somewhere close by added a sweet accompaniment. Above her head the pale light of the moon lent an idyllic glow to the underground cavern.

Right here, right now, Mindy could believe that she and Deke had escaped the tethers of the real world and traveled to a fantastical alternate universe.

Mindy took a long breath, and the scent hit her. Her heart skipped a beat and a thrill rolled through her. Leather, soap and heat. *Deke.*

Dear heavens, how could she face losing him again?

Sprout kicked her in the side. She grunted, and Deke stirred.

Mindy straightened, preparing to move away, but his arm tightened around her shoulders.

"Where are you going?" he asked sleepily.

She lifted her head. "I'm sprawled all over you. I figured you might want to change positions."

"Um, not right this minute. In fact, you may not want to move, either. You might be embarrassed."

"Why? What are you—" She stopped, because she knew what he was talking about. He was erect. The sensations her stretched-out tummy were sending her were different from her normal nonpregnant self, and so until she'd moved, she hadn't noticed.

Now that she had, the strangest feelings roiled through her. Feelings that she hadn't had for a long time. Okay, maybe she'd had them, but she hadn't acknowledged them. From the moment she'd accepted the fact that she couldn't live with Deke and his self-destructive ways, she'd done her best to curtail all of her feelings—bad and good.

She'd felt as if to admit that she was sexually frustrated was to admit that she was still in love with Deke.

So now, lying in his arms with his erection rubbing against her tummy, the feelings that had started with warmth and comfort and safety morphed into desire.

And that was ridiculous. She was over eight months pregnant. She shouldn't be feeling like this. In fact, according to all the books, she should be working up a good-size dose of resentment and irritation toward him right about now.

"What are you thinking about?" Deke asked.

Mindy's throat seized. Did she dare tell him that she was fantasizing ways they could make love on this dirt floor?

"Min? Everything okay?" He touched her chin with his fingertips and tilted her head so he could see into her eyes. When he did, his blue eyes widened slightly and his mouth quirked up.

He knew. Damn him. He always knew. Once, it had fascinated her that he could tell with a glance when she was turned on.

Now, it embarrassed her and left her feeling vulnerable. She lowered her gaze, but not in time. He made a soft growling sound deep in his throat that rumbled against her ear.

"Min, I didn't mean to get you involved in this." He spoke against her hair, his breaths warming her skin.

She nodded. "I know."

His fingers under her chin pressed harder, urging her head up again. "I'm so afraid I'll hurt you."

She opened her mouth to offer up the standard protest, but he dipped his head and stopped her words with his lips.

Dear God, she loved to kiss him. His kiss was a perfect reflection of who he was. Hard, determined, yet with an undertone of such gentleness that it made her want to cry with joy because he'd shared it with her.

She needed to stop—for her own sanity. Needed to pull back, physically and emotionally, from the precipice of sublime insanity that making love with him always plummeted her over.

He bent forward, pulling her closer, holding her mesmerized with just the touch of his mouth on hers.

She'd gotten used to the vagaries of her hormone-suffused body, but in the entire eight months she'd been pregnant she hadn't once had a lascivious thought. In fact some days she'd felt so uncomfortable and lonesome that she figured she'd never have sex again. And she'd been okay with that.

But right now—

Deke's mouth moved over hers with the confidence and strength she'd learned to depend on, until he'd proved to her that he wasn't dependable.

She kissed him back. She couldn't help herself.

He ran his thumb across the underside of her chin and then cradled her cheek in his palm. His kiss grew deeper, more intimate, more demanding. Her heart pounded and her insides thrilled as she tasted his tongue and the inside of his mouth for the first time in way too long.

Trailing his fingers down her cheekbone, he traced the line of her jaw. At the same time his lips slid across her cheek, caressing the tender skin in front of her ear. Deep within her core, a rhythmic throbbing began and grew, swelling like a symphony.

Inside her, Sprout wiggled and kicked. Her deepening arousal was disturbing him. She cradled her tummy and glanced down.

When she did. Deke pulled away. "Sorry," he muttered.

"Deke, don't."

Don't what? She couldn't answer her own question. Don't apologize? Don't stop kissing her? Don't make her remember how it felt to love him?

Ignoring the voice in her head that told her how foolish it was to go down that road, she slid her fingers around the nape of his neck and pulled him closer.

"Don't apologize," she said. "I need—" She couldn't verbalize what she needed, but he seemed to know. With a pensive, solemn expression, he sat up and shrugged out of his shearling jacket.

"Sit up for a minute," he said. When she did, he

placed the jacket behind her back, then leaned over her and kissed her again.

He was so strong. She ran her hands along the corded muscles of his forearms, shivering when she encountered the damp bandage. Then her palms slid up to trace the shape of his biceps and triceps. She lifted her head and pressed her lips against his throat, feeling the pulse thrumming there.

Balancing his weight on his arms, he lowered himself until he could nip at the curve of her jaw, at her earlobe, at the sensitive skin just beneath her ear. His breaths sawed in and out in a deep, steady rhythm that called to something visceral inside her.

"Min?" he whispered into the curve joining her neck and shoulder. "I can stop."

She shook her head. "Not yet," she murmured. "Not now."

He took in a deep breath that hitched at the top. "Then you'll have to stop me before I—before I hurt you."

She swallowed an ironic laugh. *Too late,* she thought. That ship sailed a long time ago.

Deke wanted to push away. He wanted to be the stronger one. The one who kept his head.

But he knew he was doomed to failure. He'd never been able to resist Mindy's soft, full mouth or her sexy, made-for-loving body. Or the sweet way she always made him feel like a hero, even though they both knew he was anything but.

They'd been together since junior year in high school. They'd been lovers since graduation night. She knew everything about him.

She knew where he liked to be kissed, to be touched.

She knew how to bring him to the point of no return with nothing more than a brief caress of her fingers. She knew that although he'd never admit it to any of his buddies, he loved for her to touch his nipples. The sharp, erotic sensation of her fingertips and nails on them nearly sent him over the edge.

As if she knew what he was thinking, she slid her palms down his biceps and over his pectorals. Then she rubbed his nipples until they stood erect. He gasped, and she chuckled.

Okay, then. He knew everything about her, too. This would be tit for tat.

Like right now. He buried his nose in the little curve between her neck and her shoulder. If he ran his tongue along the apex of her shoulder, right over the little bump covered by golden skin, she'd moan and squirm.

He did.

And she did.

His throat closed with laughter—and sweet, aching nostalgia. Her hands tightened around his muscled wrists. Absently, he remembered that her fingers didn't reach all the way around.

He shifted his weight to his left arm and began unbuttoning the buttons at the top of her sweater. He didn't dare look up. He was afraid of what he'd see in her eyes.

Excitement, anticipation or apprehension?

When she pushed his hands away, his heart sank all the way to his boots. His logical brain, however, reminded his heart that they were in this place because she was in danger, and it was all because of him.

He had no right to take advantage of her. She was at his mercy. Dependent on him for safety, for comfort, for strength—for her very life.

Which made her vulnerable. And he was exploiting that vulnerability by letting his body overrule his brain. What he needed to be doing right now was figuring out their next move.

He knew perfectly well what this idyllic refuge was that they had found. It was bait—to lure them into a false sense of security.

Novus Ordo was still out there and still plotting to wear him down, still playing cat and mouse. For the moment he'd lifted his paw, giving them a taste of freedom—a false belief that they had a chance to escape. As soon as they tried, he'd clamp down on them again.

Her fingers brushed across his again, reminding him that his hand was resting near her breasts. He pulled away, but she stopped him. He watched with bated breath as she guided his palm to her waist, and then slid it up until his fingers curved around the bulge of her tummy. Against his palm, her satin-smooth skin seemed to vibrate with life—hers and the life of the tiny child inside her.

He closed his eyes, and for a moment he existed only in the sensations that flowed through the nerve endings on his fingertips and palms. He didn't think he'd ever felt anything so alive, so vibrant, so awesome.

To his surprise, tears stung his eyes, so he lowered his head, unwilling to let her see his weakness. He'd never even dreamed of being a father, never once considered that a precious, innocent child could spring from these loins of his. From the same DNA that had produced his cruel dad, and himself.

He pressed his forehead against the warm bulge of her tummy and silently prayed that one day he might be worthy of her and her baby.

He felt the tears leaking out from beneath his lids. He couldn't let her feel the salty drops on her skin. He hadn't cried since he was in junior high school and his dad had showed him what happened to crybabies.

So, under the pretense of nuzzling her tummy, he managed to wipe his eyes on the tail of her sweater.

Her abdomen moved as she sighed. Her fingers tightened around his, and she slid his hand across the slope of her tummy and farther up, toward her breasts.

His breath hitched and he raised his gaze. "Mindy—"

"Hush, Deke," she whispered. "Please don't spoil this with logic and reason. It's nothing more than a moment stolen out of time. It's not like we've never done it before." She made a quick head gesture toward her tummy.

"But you're—"

She put her fingers to his lips. "Shh. Don't even go there. Please don't *think*. For once in your life, just feel. I need you to take me somewhere outside of here. Outside of myself, because if I keep worrying about what's going to happen, I'll go insane."

As she talked, she continued to slide his hand upward, to the underside of her breast. Then she gripped his wrist and guided him over the fullest part to the peak, pressing his fingers to her nipple. She gasped.

And sighed again.

Deke's first instinct was to jerk his hand away. She was pregnant. These weren't the small delicate breasts he'd teased and nuzzled so many times. These were big breasts, pregnant breasts. They were firm and full, and the nipple was large and erect, waiting for the hungry little mouth of her son.

Their son.

His body instantly hardened—muscles, tendons, bones—all stiffened in sharp, aching hunger. His mouth watered to taste the distended tip.

He caressed the nipple with the gentle touch of his fingers. As he did it hardened and puckered in reaction, and Mindy's breathing ratcheted up a notch. She blew air softly in and out, and her body writhed and arched the tiniest bit, revealing her yearning for more of what he offered.

So he cradled her full round globe in his hand, kneading and squeezing, then running his thumb across and around her ever-tightening nipple. His erection grew harder, longer, as his body throbbed in familiar reaction to her obvious need and desire. Turning her on had always fed his own desire.

But this—what he felt right now—was a level of longing he'd never before experienced. Not even when they were horny teenagers, searching for a place where they could be alone together.

"How—how does it feel?" he asked with trepidation. "To be pregnant?"

Mindy put her hand on top of his. It had always awed her how much bigger his hand was than hers. "It's really strange. Different every day."

She looked at the man who'd created this baby with her. He was so scared. She could read the fear in his face. Over the years she'd known him, she'd watched him forge himself into a warrior. He'd taught himself not to be afraid of anything. Yet this small, helpless life within her terrified him.

"He feels like you," she whispered, her voice catching. "It's like I have a part of you inside me all the time."

She'd known that, deep inside, but she'd never said

the words, not even to herself. Now she understood the erotic dreams that woke her deep in the night. Now the indescribable longings she'd never acknowledged in daylight had a source. And the source was Deke.

He made a deep, throaty sound, and a shudder rumbled through him. His erection pulsed against her thigh.

Instantly, her body tightened in desire and in the deepest, most intimate part of her, a sweet familiar throbbing began.

Deke continued caressing the tip of her breast as he lifted his head. He leaned forward until his mouth brushed hers.

Then he kissed her. A desperate, deep, soul-searching kiss. As his mouth took hers, she whimpered in uncontrollable response.

He froze.

She moaned in frustration as he pulled away.

"What's wrong?" she whispered.

"I'm hurting you."

"Deke, believe me, you're not." Mindy's breasts, her center, burned with frustration. "Please." She wrapped her hand around the nape of his neck and pulled his head toward her. "Don't stop."

And he didn't. He kissed her over and over, tasting her as if it were the first time. She was as sexy to him as she'd always been. Maybe more so. Something, whether it was her pregnancy or just the fact that it had been so long, had him so turned on that he was afraid he might explode like a horny kid. He pulled back, trying to control himself, but Mindy moaned in protest. She caught his hand and brought it to the apex of her thighs.

He felt her heat, even beneath the wool pants she wore. And when he pressed his palm against her, her already labored breathing sped up.

"Deke," she whispered, then gasped again. "Oh!" Her hand covered his, and she pressed down against his palm.

He listened to her shallow, rhythmic breaths, her small cries. And clenched his teeth to keep from following her climax with his own.

"Deke," she finally breathed. "Don't run away. Let me—" She reached for his pants zipper.

"No. This isn't a good idea."

"Why?" She clasped his hand in hers and brought his palm to her lips. She chuckled, still feeling the small aftershocks of her climax. "It's not like you can get me *more* pregnant."

As soon as the words were out of her mouth, she knew she'd screwed up. Royally.

Deke pushed away and sat up. "Nope," he rasped, as he pushed his fingers through his shaggy hair. "Apparently that was one time I managed to deliver maximum damage on the first try."

"Deke, wait. I'm sorry."

"For what? Getting pregnant? That wasn't your fault." He rubbed his eyes, then swiped a hand across his face. "It was your mother's funeral. I took advantage of your grief."

"You did not! It just happened. In fact, if I hadn't kissed you, you'd have been out of there like a cat with its tail on fire." She smiled briefly. "Trust me, Deke. I do not regret being pregnant."

"I do."

She flinched and her eyes pricked with tears at his

quick, simple declaration. But she had known this was how he would feel. From the first moment she'd realized that she was pregnant, there had been no question in her mind.

She'd wanted the baby, whether Deke did or not.

Gingerly, as if he were a skittish colt, she took his hand and pressed it against her tummy.

"Can you regret this? He's your son, Deke. A part of you and me. If we're lucky, the best parts."

"And if we're not lucky?" He was thinking of his father.

"Trust me. In this we're lucky."

"Good to know," he muttered. "When we get out of here, remind me to buy a lottery ticket." He stared at his hand where it rested on her stomach. He still seemed awestruck—and terrified—by her pregnancy.

"Don't make fun of me. You have no idea how beautiful, how sexy you make me feel. I haven't felt either for months. Come back and lie down with me," she said. "I'm cold."

He scooted back over and reclined against the warm dirt wall, positioning himself so that she leaned against his left side.

She pressed her hand against his chest and tucked her head into the snug, sweet place between his neck and shoulder.

"This feels good," she whispered. "Like home."

Deke grimaced at her sleepy words and tightened his arm around her shoulders.

"Deke?" she whispered.

"Yeah, sugar?"

"What time do you think it is? And what day?"

It was a good question. He'd tried his best to keep

up with the time. "It's dark. I'd guess it might be around midnight. Best I can figure, it's Thursday night. Or Friday morning."

He bent his head and pressed a kiss against her hair. "Sleep, Min. I'll keep you safe." He leaned his head back against the hard dirt wall and stared at the starlit sky through the opening high above their heads. He felt her breasts rise and fall with her breaths, heard them slow and even out as she dozed.

The immediacy and strength of Mindy's response to him awed him—and terrified him.

He hadn't meant to lose control of himself, or get caught up in her growing reaction to his caresses.

All he'd wanted to do was taste, just for a moment, the sweetness of her kisses, feel the lovely soft firmness of her skin.

He hadn't meant to turn her on.

The thought sent a shudder of erotic thrill through him. He grimaced and shifted uncomfortably. He could easily and quickly take care of his discomfort, but he'd promised Mindy he'd keep her safe. He wasn't going to take the slightest risk of being distracted, not even for a moment.

Besides, from the very first time he'd touched her, when they'd both been innocent teens, he'd never known anything that fueled his own desire as much as stoking the fires of hers did.

She'd thanked him, but in truth she'd turned herself on. In doing so she'd turned him on, too. He'd gotten as much—well, almost as much—satisfaction as she had.

His eyes slowly closed, and his thoughts began to wander. He clamped his jaw. He couldn't sleep. He needed to keep lookout.

He couldn't do anything about the signs they'd left at the campfire. Probably didn't matter, anyway. Novus knew they were here. He'd probably arranged for the kindling and candles.

Deke snorted. If there hadn't been any fish in the spring, he'd have probably arranged for them, too.

He looked down at the top of Mindy's head. She was asleep in his arms, trusting him to keep her safe.

Anger, hot as a flash fire, whooshed through him. It took every ounce of his strength to stay still.

Why don't you just come and get me? he wanted to stand up and shout. *Come on, Novus. Show your face. Fight it out, fair and square, like a man.*

He doubted they'd managed to wire the entire mine, so he'd probably be yelling to deaf ears, but it would sure make him feel better.

I know why you won't face me, you scumbag. You're no man. You're a coward. Just like your wormy outlaw brother. Frank James. Give me a break! Covering up your weaselly face with a mask! Just like your boss Novus.

"I'll be damned—!" *Just like Novus.* The significance of his comparison slammed him in the gut. He clamped his jaw and took long, even breaths, trying to slow his suddenly racing heart. Trying not to disturb Mindy.

Could that be it? Could this guy, obviously American, actually be the brother of Novus Ordo? Deke knew from Rook's description and the forensic artist's rendering he'd seen that the terrorist was medium height and skinny with a narrow face and beady eyes. And Rook had sworn that Novus, whose messages were always delivered on CD in a heavy, Middle Eastern accent, was actually American.

It would explain everything. Novus's obsessive need to hide his face. Frank James affecting that ridiculous bandanna. It might be a leap, but it made sense.

Why else would James hide his face? Deke knew the weasel didn't intend to let either Mindy or himself get out of there alive.

Deke cursed silently. He had information that could bring Novus down, and he had no way to get a message out.

Rook, you sonofabitch! I need you, man. More than I ever have before. Between us, we'd figure out who Novus is and bring him and his brother down.

"Deke?" Mindy lifted her head. "What's the matter?"

Damn it, he'd woken her. "Nothing, sugar. Go to sleep."

She shifted. "Did you hear something?"

He shook his head and cradled the back of her head in his palm. "Nope. Just thinking."

She laid her hand on his chest. "Must have been some kind of thinking, to send your heart racing like that. What were you thinking about?"

"Novus," he said reluctantly. He didn't want her to know his fears. On the other hand, he owed her the truth. He'd gotten her into this. He probably should tell her exactly what and who they were battling.

"How we ended up here. It started out innocently enough. Irina's accountant gave her final warning. He'd apparently talked with her a few times before about her depleted funds. But this time he warned her that if she continued the same level of spending for another three to four months, she'd be bankrupt. Irina had to make a decision. Shut down BHSAR or stop spending a fortune searching for Rook. She made the only decision she could."

"I still don't understand why she gave up. They were more in love than any two people I've ever met. If I were Irina, the only way I'd ever give up is if I saw the body."

Deke tried to suppress the thought that sprang to the front of his mind.

So your definition of giving up doesn't include divorce?

He bit his tongue until the urge to lash out at her for leaving him went away. Hell, he knew he'd been an ass and had hurt her in too many ways to count, but it still hurt that she'd done the very thing he'd expected her—that he'd pushed her—to do.

He clenched his jaw and continued his explanation. "When Rook left the air force, he still had his burning desire to rescue the innocent. Black Hills Search and Rescue was his baby. Irina knew that Rook would never want to give up his dream. So she made the choice he'd have wanted her to make."

He felt Mindy's shoulder quiver and heard her swallow a sob. "Min? You okay?"

She nodded against his shoulder. "It's just so sad."

"Yeah. Apparently, as soon as Irina stopped searching, rumors started circulating that she'd found him. The first indication we got was from Homeland Security, reporting on the increased international chatter. Especially in the regions around the corridor that joins Pakistan, China and Afghanistan. A small province called Mahjidastan."

"Where you were shot down."

He nodded. "Novus Ordo's headquarters."

Mindy pushed herself up to a sitting position, groaning with the effort. Deke moved to help her. "So Novus found out that Irina had stopped the search."

"Matt left Mahjidastan within six hours after Irina called him—on the first flight he could get. He was followed. Then as soon as he got back, Aimee Vick's baby was kidnapped. That means that Novus knew what Irina had done *before* the chatter started."

"But how—"

"Only one way. We've got a traitor inside BHSAR."

"Oh my God, Deke. Who? Don't you know everyone?"

"I know the BHSAR team. I've met the rest of the staff. Don't know much about them. But the traitor has to be someone who knows everything that goes on. The specialists, Irina's personal assistant, her lawyer—"

"That's—what? Five people."

"Six, if I don't count Matt. Aaron Gold, Brock O'Neill, Rafe Jackson, Pam Jameison, Richards the lawyer, and maybe her accountant."

"I forgot about Rafe Jackson. I've never met him. Which one could do something like this?"

Deke shook his head. "Before all this started, I'd have said none of them. But now—everybody on the team, especially Irina, is in danger because I didn't identify a traitor in our midst. Think about it. They've already sabotaged my bird. Almost cost Matt and Aimee and her baby their lives."

Mindy considered the few times she'd met the other members of the team. "Brock's awfully secretive."

"Yeah, but can you see him betraying his country?"

"Maybe he doesn't consider it his country. He's Sioux, right? We destroyed *his* country."

Deke frowned at her.

"Or Aaron Gold? I only met him a couple of times."

"His dad was in the air force with Rook. He died a hero. Aaron was thrilled to be asked to join the BHSAR team."

"And Rafe Jackson?"

Deke didn't speak for a moment. "Rafe was born in England, but he went to a lot of trouble to become an American citizen."

"He's British?"

"Actually, his mother is from Saudi Arabia. His name is Rafiq."

"Wow. Any one of them could be the traitor."

Deke shook his head. "I guess you're right."

"What did you tell them about coming here to rescue me? I mean, if one of them is working with Novus, they know what's going on here."

"Let's just say I took precautions."

"What kind of precautions? What could you do to be sure the terrorist didn't find out vital information?"

"I'd rather not say."

"Really? Here, too?" Mindy craned her neck to look around.

"I have no idea. I just don't want to take any chances."

"So all this—it's because Novus is trying to find Rook, when he doesn't even know if he's alive? I guess whoever shot Rook didn't have the luxury of hanging around to make sure he died."

Deke sighed. "Guess not."

"Why don't they just go after you? Or Irina?"

"He can't get to us directly, and he knows that. There's too much security at the ranch. And it's the same reason he didn't just grab Matt. One of *us* disappearing would create an international incident, just like Rook's disappearance did. Since we're still connected with the military."

"So instead, he's grabbing those close to you."

Deke squeezed his eyes shut and rubbed his temple. "Something like that."

"Why? What's he after?"

"He's doing everything he can to be sure Rook can't identify him. You've seen the mask that Novus Ordo always wears?

"Sure. I've seen the pictures they've shown on the news shows. It looks like those green and white disposable surgical masks you can buy in any drugstore." She uttered a short laugh. "He looks pretty ridiculous."

"Yeah, well, they've been effective. For several years, he's been the most famous and most dangerous terrorist on the planet. The mask fascinates people. It makes him look mysterious."

"And nobody's ever seen his face?"

"That's the word. No one except his most trusted inner circle. And Rook." Deke's gut twisted at his friend's name. Rook had taken Deke under his wing on the first day of first grade. He was only a few months older, but he'd always been the stronger one, the more courageous one, the leader. Rook had been born to lead, and Deke had been perfectly happy to be his sidekick.

"He saw him when he rescued you."

He looked at her, surprised.

"Rook told me. He said you saved Travis Ronson's life."

He'd never wanted her to know about that. Perversely, he would rather have her believe he didn't love her anymore.

The truth, that his helicopter had been shot down, which provided the means for Rook's team to find Novus, painted him in a sympathetic light that he didn't deserve.

"I only found out all that afterwards. The way Rook tells it, he and his team hit their camp at night while most of Novus's men were sleeping. He found the camp by using the GPS locator in my shoulder."

"In your shoulder? Is it still there?"

"No." He reached with his right hand to touch the little bump where the small chip was located, but the movement made his inflamed wound sting so he stopped. "The battery only lasts about a year. Still itches, though."

"So Rook rescued you."

"The team did. While they were transporting me to the helicopter, Rook took out a couple of guards with a silenced handgun, and found himself face-to-face with Novus, mask and all. Then a gust of wind ripped the mask right off him. Rook said he got an extreme close-up view before Novus covered his face with his arm."

"Oh my God! He saw Novus Ordo's face."

"Then two more guards tackled him. He almost didn't get away. One of them grabbed his dog tags and tried to choke him. About that time Brock O'Neill took out the other one with a machine gun. They got to the helicopter just as it was lifting off. Another few seconds and one of Novus's machine guns or flamethrowers could have grounded it. Then everybody would be dead." He wiped a hand down his face. "Truth is, it's my fault Novus targeted Rook."

Mindy shuddered. "What did Rook say about Novus? What did he look like?"

Deke laid his head back against the dirt wall. His mouth lifted at one corner. "That's classified."

"Right. Classified. Does Irina know?"

He frowned. "Probably."

"Do you think she's more trustworthy than me?"

"No. But—"

"Then tell me. You've always said how important it is to know your enemy. Well, I need to know my enemy, too."

He sent her a pensive look. "Okay. The latest, greatest, most infamous terrorist on the planet is American."

Chapter Eight

"Novus Ordo is American? No way!" Mindy stared at Deke, stunned. His head still rested against the wall behind him. He swallowed, and his Adam's apple moved up and down. The tendons in his neck and the muscles that joined his neck and shoulder stood out as sharp shadows. Dear heavens, there was nothing about him that wasn't sexy. Even his neck. Even his Adam's apple.

Deke smiled and her heart gave a little leap at the curve of his lips. "Way."

"Is— Was Rook sure? What did he tell you he looked like?"

"Rook said he was kind of ordinary looking, maybe of Irish or Scottish or British ancestry. But get this. He heard him curse, in a very American accent."

"Deke, this is unbelievable. Why would an American—?" She stopped. It was a silly and useless question. There had been other Americans who'd turned against their country. "But the audio recordings he's sent to the media have all been heavily accented English."

"Right. You notice he's never sent a video. Homeland Security's theory is that one of his inner circle makes the recordings for him. Plus Rook worked with a computer facial recognition analyst for the CIA. For the past two years the CIA and Homeland Security have been trying to find a match to fit his description."

"Have you seen it? The sketch?"

Deke nodded. "Average-looking guy. Medium height. Bordering on skinny. Long nose, close-set eyes, sharp chin."

Disturbingly similar to Frank James. The cowboy outfit and bandanna mask couldn't hide James's slender build, his beady eyes or his narrow face. With every passing minute, Deke was more convinced that James was Novus's brother, since, based on the sketch, he was too old to be his son.

Deke wasn't naive enough to think that Novus would be here carrying out this witch hunt himself, but he could easily believe that Novus's brother would do it. Hell, the sketch could be of Frank James himself.

He wondered what their real names were, and if they were born and reared in this part of the country or had located here because of Rook.

At least he had information that Novus didn't know he had, and he would guard that information with his life. It might be a way to bring Novus down.

"Deke?"

Mindy had asked him a question. "What?"

"What did Rook say about Novus's hair color? Was he dark or fair?"

"Rook couldn't see his hair because of his shemagh, but he said the CGI expert did a great job on the face."

"Shemagh?"

"That's the traditional Arabian headdress. Novus wears it on his head, but doesn't use it to cover his face. He uses the surgical mask for that."

"So none of you recognized the sketch? You'd never seen him before?"

"Nope."

"And the CIA has no idea who he is?"

He shook his head. "They've been going over all reports of missing Caucasian males from the past ten or so years, starting with the first known reports of Novus Ordo's involvement in terrorism."

Mindy felt like she'd woken up in the middle of a movie—a thriller. She couldn't keep up with everything Deke was telling her. She was still processing his astonishing statement: *Novus Ordo is American.*

More specifically, she was processing the realization that Deke knew so much about international terrorist activities, Novus Ordo and what sounded like classified government secrets.

He hadn't been kidding when he'd said *it's classified.* He had just told her a secret of global importance.

A sudden sense of overwhelming responsibility weighed on her shoulders. It was crushing. Suffocating. She put a hand to her breastbone as her pulse hammered in her ears. "Oh."

"Mindy? Is it the baby?"

She shook her head. "It's just—I almost wish you hadn't told me."

"I know what you mean. But after everything I've put you through, I figured you deserved to know. I can trust you not to tell anyone, can't I?"

"Of course you can. Deke, is *this* what you do? What you've been doing since you got back from Mahjidastan? You're a—a secret government agent? Some kind of covert operative?"

He laughed, but he sounded more ironic than

amused. "No. BHSAR isn't a secret government agency. It's what Rook wanted it to be. A private search-and-rescue company that does as many volunteer rescues as paid jobs, if not more."

"A private company. So, what were you doing over there spying on Novus Ordo?"

"That was supposed to be a one-time thing. A personal favor asked of him by—" he paused and drew in a long breath "—by a friend."

A very high-placed, influential friend. Mindy had no doubt those were the words Deke hadn't said.

"If I hadn't gotten shot down…if Rook hadn't seen Novus's face…" He shrugged. "Once all this is over, we should be able to do what we thought we'd done years ago. Be private citizens who just happen to run a local search-and-rescue operation."

"With an occasional favor for a special friend or two."

Deke just shrugged and quirked up the corner of his mouth.

"I don't know how you've managed to stay sane."

Another harsh laugh. "Maybe I haven't."

"Oh, I think you're much stronger than you realize." Mindy lay back against the softness of Deke's shearling jacket.

"Yeah? Have you decided I'm not broken?"

The question sounded ironic, but Mindy heard an undertone that she'd never heard in his voice before—an anxiousness, as if the answer she gave to that question was very important to him.

"Hmm. I think most of your life you've looked at strength in the wrong way. You equate strength with rigidity. And that's dangerous. You don't need to be too strong to break. If you're rigid, then you can't bend. And if you can't bend, you're doomed to break." She yawned. "Or something like that..."

"And bending. How is that a good thing? Isn't it like bowing down?"

She opened one eye and squinted at him. "No. It means you're resilient. You can take punishment without breaking. You'll be beaten down, but you'll spring back again."

A deep laugh rumbled through his chest. "You're exhausted. You need to get some sleep," Deke murmured.

"I'm not sure if I'll ever sleep again..." Her words faded.

"Oh, I think you will." He leaned over and pressed a kiss against her forehead. "I'm going to get up and take a look around, okay?"

"You need to sleep, too." She was already drifting off. *Sprout, don't you dare decide to be born until we get out of here. You can hold off another day or so, right?*

"I'll wait. I've gone without sleep for longer than this and survived. If you need me, call me."

"My hero," she whispered.

Deke slid carefully away from Mindy just as a deep rumble echoed through the cavern.

Mindy jerked and Deke stiffened.

That was an explosion. What the hell?

"What was that?" Mindy asked, worry lacing her voice.

"Thunder." Deke winced at his lie. "Go back to sleep. Even if it rains, we're protected here."

He rose to his feet and looked down at her. She'd already drifted back to sleep. She was so pretty, so young, so trusting, looking with her eyes closed and her face relaxed in sleep. Her silky-smooth hair fell across her cheek like chocolate-colored velvet.

God, I know I don't deserve to have a prayer answered, but don't make her suffer for my screwups. Please don't let her die.

What had gone so wrong? How had he let her get caught up in the train wreck that was his life? She didn't deserve this. She deserved a safe, stable home with all the special things that came with it: a husband who loved her and put her safety above everything else; beautiful, smart children she could be proud of; a life free of fear and danger.

The kind of life he could never give her.

His fists clenched as he turned away. It hurt his heart too much to look at her for very long. Especially like she was now. Innocent, vulnerable, trusting enough to sleep peacefully. It didn't seem to bother her that she had no one but him to protect her.

He should have brought backup. Rafe had been available, as had Aaron. But even if he'd trusted them enough, it would have been a fatal mistake. Novus had demanded that he come alone. He'd given him no choice. Out here on this lonely stretch of prairie, a second car or a second body would have been immediately noticeable. They could have been killed.

He fingered the bump on his shoulder. He hadn't told Mindy a complete lie. His scar did itch, partly because of the previous transmitter, but partly because of the new one. Who knew if it would prove useful, especially if they stayed underground. But he was glad he had it. He only wished he had some sort of two-way communication device.

If he stood directly under the ventilation shaft at exactly the right time, there might be a chance that one of the specialists would pick up on the chip's location. He needed to let someone know that Mindy was eight months pregnant. But he had no way to get the information out.

He should have hidden a two-way transmitter somewhere on him. But hell, they'd searched him. He was damn lucky they didn't get around to checking his boots.

Why hadn't he taken steps to protect Mindy from Novus like he had Irina?

Because he'd been clinging to the hope that after two years she was no longer close enough to him to be in danger. It was a stupid assumption.

Deke stood under the ventilation shaft as he argued with himself. And then argued with himself about the futility of arguing with himself. Finally, he stopped at the far end of the lagoon and stared at the coal-car rails that plummeted down the steep incline.

They couldn't go that way. He could make it on foot if he were alone, but Mindy would never be able to stay on her feet. The incline was about twenty degrees, which didn't sound like much, but in her condition she had enough trouble walking on level ground.

It amazed him that the heavily loaded coal cars had managed to stay on the tracks, especially if the tracks curved.

He did an about-face, just as another rumble shook the ground. Again, he held his breath. But nothing else happened. After another few seconds, the rumble faded.

He swallowed heavily. Those were explosions, not

thunder. And he'd bet money he knew what was being blown up.

The mine tunnels. James was trapping them in here. And there were only two reasons he would do that. Either he was ensuring that the only way out was back through the hotel, or— Deke did not want to think about the second reason. But he had to.

Or James was sealing them inside the mine before he killed them.

But why do that when he could just man the exits?

Good question. Maybe Novus didn't have as many men at his disposal as Deke had assumed he had. Maybe James was blowing up the tunnels because he couldn't guard them all at once.

If that was the case, then maybe Deke could get the upper hand after all. He figured he could handle two-to-one odds—maybe even three to one.

He turned to stare at the other end of the tracks, wondering if one of the explosions had caved in that tunnel. With a shrug, he continued his analysis of the best way to proceed. It was something to do at least.

The upper incline was much shallower—nearly level. If he were Novus, he'd discard that incline and the branch tunnel that led back to the hotel. Those were the easy choices.

But then, if Deke was thinking about taking the most difficult tunnel, even with a pregnant woman in tow, then Novus would also think about it.

He sighed and rubbed his temples. His thoughts were whirling out of control. Probably the result of too little food and sleep, and too many zaps with James's fancy Taser. At least the racing thoughts had distracted him from his other problem—his frustrated libido. He dropped to his haunches and winced at the pressure of the denim on his not-quite-deflated erection. Okay, he wasn't totally distracted.

He dipped his hands into the cold spring and splashed water on his face. Then, sitting back on his heels, he let his gaze wander around the large room. The only sounds that reached his ears were the soft trilling of the spring and an almost inaudible whistle of wind from the ventilation shaft high above.

He massaged the back of his neck. Much as he would have liked to catch a few winks of sleep, he needed to search the area for anything he could use as a weapon.

With a tired groan, he rose to his feet and went searching. The first thing he wanted to do was check out that blanket on the man car. If it wasn't too filthy, Mindy could cover up with it. He was sure that she was going to get cold before the night was over.

He crossed the shallow spring and approached the vehicle. A quick inspection told him that not only was the wool blanket filthy and moth-eaten, it was mildewed, as well. It wouldn't be healthy for Mindy to wrap up in it.

Gingerly, he pulled the thing off the car and peered over the sides, holding the lantern high in the air.

He froze.

Dynamite. Old dynamite. Several bundles of it. And from the little he knew about it, old meant dangerous. Carefully, holding his breath, he lowered the lantern enough to get a good look at the sticks without letting the lantern's heat come close to it.

The first thing he noticed once the vehicles floor was illuminated was a tangle of blasting caps. Dozens of them. The second thing he noticed was the bright spots on the surface of the sticks.

Crystals. Ah, hell. Those crystals were pure nitroglycerine. A bump—even a slight movement, could cause them to explode.

Hardly daring to breathe, he backed away from the car. Was that dynamite set to explode? He held the lantern up, searching to see if there was a fuse running from the car. But he didn't see anything.

So he crouched down, checking underneath, and walked all the way around, but he didn't see a fuse there, either. He did, however, find a crowbar leaning against the wall behind the car. Grabbing it, he straightened, blowing his breath out in a sigh. Maybe the dynamite hadn't been rigged by James. Maybe it had just been stored there for the past fifty or so years.

Still, the question remained. Did James know it was here?

It hardly mattered. They couldn't go near that car. They couldn't even breathe on it, or the nitroglycerine might blow. He headed back toward the alcove, testing the crowbar in his hands.

He crouched at the spring and scooped another couple of handfuls of water into his mouth, then sat back under the shaft and took his first deep breath since discovering the dynamite. He knew one thing for certain. They had to get out of here as soon as possible. In the meantime, on the minuscule chance that a satellite was in range and anyone might be monitoring transmissions, he'd stay under the opening as long as he could.

DEKE WOKE UP. HE'D HEARD something besides the quiet sound of burbling water.

There it was again. A quiet moan.

Mindy!

He vaulted to his feet, swaying a little as the blood rushed away from his head, and ran to the alcove.

She was sitting up, her hands pressed against her stomach.

"Min? What is it?"

"I don't kn—" Her whole body stiffened, and a sharp gasp cut off her words. "There's something—wrong."

Deke sat and took her hands in his. "What can I do?"

She shook her head. Even in the dim light of dawn seeping in through the ventilation shaft, he could see how pale her face was.

"Hey," he said, keeping his voice as calm as he could. He squeezed her fingers gently. "I'm pretty sure you're supposed to breathe."

She looked up at him. "So now you know all about pregnancy?" Her voice was strained, belying the lightness of her words.

"I took a course."

"Nice to know."

She pushed a breath out through pursed lips. Then drew in another. Taking them long and slow.

"That's good. Good, Min." He brought her hands to his mouth and kissed her knuckles, buying some time as he racked his brain. He *had* taken a course years ago, during his air force training. It had included an overview of delivering a baby. A *brief* overview.

Dear God, please don't let this baby come now. There was no way he could keep a newborn infant safe. No way he could take care of Mindy.

Focus. What were the signs of labor? *Contractions,* he answered himself.

"Are you hurting?" he asked.

She shook her head. "Not now."

He nodded. "So that wasn't a contraction?"

Mindy closed her eyes and flattened her lips. "No. It was a contraction, all right. And I don't think it was the first one."

Deke's training was coming back to him. Beads of sweat prickled his forehead and the nape of his neck. "How—how far apart are they?"

"I don't know. They started in my sleep. I was having a little back pain. And once or twice I felt a cramp. I palpated my abdomen. The uterus is definitely contracting."

"I didn't understand most of that, but you're the nurse, so I'll take your word for it."

She sent him a wan smile. "Thanks."

"Is this—" he made a vague gesture toward her tummy "—is this it? Are you having the baby?"

"No." Mindy lifted her chin. "No. It's too early. And—look where we are. No. My baby will *not* be born here." She cradled her tummy. "Did you hear me, Sprout? Stay in there. We'll be home soon."

My baby. Those two words echoed in his ears. She'd told him that the baby was his. She'd even referred to him as *our baby* a few times. He was surprised how much it hurt to hear her say *my* instead of *our* right now.

He cleared his throat. "What can I do to help?"

Her olive-green eyes met his gaze. "Go find a way out of here, get help and come back and rescue me."

"Forget that. I'm not leaving you here. Especially if you're having the baby." And especially since he knew they were practically sitting on enough dynamite to blow the entire mine.

She glared at him. "I am not having the baby."

Despite the seriousness of their situation, her determination made him smile. "What? You're going to stop him from being born with your steely resolve?"

"Damn straight I will." She stuck her chin out pugnaciously.

"And you call me stubborn," he muttered under his breath.

"I heard tha— Oh!"

"Min?" He took her hand and squeezed it reassuringly. Her fingers tightened around his with surprising strength. "Breathe, sugar."

She kept a stranglehold on his fingers until the contraction was over. He spent the time watching her, and estimating how long it had been between contractions.

"I think it's been ten minutes since the first contraction," he said, as she pushed herself back against the dirt wall.

She nodded. "That's what I thought. Ten minutes apart. I'm in premature labor."

"Is that some kind of labor that comes before real labor?" he asked hopefully. He had a sinking feeling that the answer to that question was no.

Sure enough, she shook her head. His heart sank and his pulse sped up.

"It's real labor, but it'll go away. Like I told you, it's too early. He's not due to make his appearance for six more weeks." She pushed herself up a little more. "Can you bring me some water?"

Deke fetched her a bucket of water. She drank several swallows.

"I've got to lie down," she told him. "The recommendation for slowing or stopping premature contractions is to lie still for a couple of hours and drink lots of water. That's the best chance I have to stop them."

"Okay, so we'll wait for two hours, then we'll both get out of here."

Mindy shook her head. "I don't think I'll be able to walk. Not in two hours. I'd just go back into labor." She put her hand on his. "Deke, you've got to find the way out."

"No. I'm not leaving you."

She maneuvered herself into a reclining position and turned onto her left side.

"This is no time to start being sentimental," she said. "I need you to do what you do best. What would you do if I were an injured man? Or a female innocent you were sent in to rescue?"

He scowled at her. "You're not."

She scowled right back at him.

He relented. "I'd leave the man with a weapon to defend himself while I scouted the best way out. I'd probably carry the female out with me."

"You can't. You're injured, and I'm not only too heavy, I can't walk."

"I can't leave you here, alone and helpless."

"It's the only way. Now give me the knife and go find us a way out."

He silently handed the knife over to her.

"I know you've already figured out what Novus is doing," she said.

He nodded. "He's got all the exits manned, and he's figured out what he thinks I'm going to do. I'm telling you, he's got a time frame he's working within. As soon as he can figure out a way to get to Irina—" He stopped. He didn't want to tell her that Novus's timeline included killing the two of them as soon as he got his hands on Irina Castle.

"He's having fun trying to anticipate my next move. His favorite thing to do is toy with people."

"Like a cat with a mouse."

"And like that cat, he knows exactly when and how he's going to go in for the kill."

EVERYTHING WAS ABOUT CHOICE.

Deke had to give Novus credit. James had said Novus's goal was to wear him down. And as bad as he hated to admit it, Novus was accomplishing his goal. Because right now, Deke was just about at the end of his rope.

He was tired. He was weak and nauseated from loss of blood and the fever brought on by his wound. And he hadn't slept more than an hour in the last twenty-four.

Now, he'd literally come to the end of the line. He sat on his haunches and stared at the pile of rock and broken timbers in front of him. Dark shadows danced in the lantern's light, and the burbling of the spring mocked him. Every few seconds, a silvery reflection in the water caught his eye. The little fish, battling their way through the rocks to swim downstream.

Toward Mindy.

He thought about her, back in that alcove alone where he'd left her over an hour ago. That had been a bad choice. The fact that it was the only choice didn't make it good.

And now he was staring at the result of the rumbling he'd heard, the rumbling he'd told her was thunder. He knew the cave-in he was staring at had been caused by the explosion, because here and there, wisps of smoke still rose from the debris, and the hot smell of explosive and ozone permeated the air.

He'd tried to dig through the debris in a couple of places using the crowbar, but he hadn't gotten very far. All he'd managed to do was start a couple of small rock slides and stir up a fog of hot, choking smoke and dust. He couldn't take the chance of tumbling the whole wall of rocks and timbers down on his head.

So he had no choice here, either. He had to go back.

But what was he going back to? Another dead end and the choice of lying to Mindy or telling her the truth, that they were trapped in the mine?

Because if James had blown this tunnel then he'd blown the downhill one, too. It confirmed his suspicion that James didn't have enough men to guard every exit.

One thing in their favor. Maybe.

He cupped his left hand and scooped up water to drink, then bent down and splashed some on his face. After swiping the water from his eyes, he picked up the lantern and the crowbar and turned on his heel.

MINDY JERKED AWAKE. She'd heard something.

Dear God, let it be Deke.

She winced as her little Sprout kicked her, reminding her that he'd been asleep, too.

Holding her breath, she listened. There it was again. The noise that had woken her. And this time she knew what it was.

The crunch of footsteps on dirt and gravel.

Not Deke. Her pulse skittered, stealing her breath. Deke would have already called out to her.

As quietly as she could, she scooted farther back

against the farthest wall of the alcove, pulling the knife from her bra.

She stared at the dim glow that outlined the alcove's opening, doing her best to keep her breathing steady. The knife's handle was warm from her body heat, and although she'd seen the damage it could do, right now it felt pitifully small.

Then the light at the entrance changed, brightened.

Her breath hitched. Whoever it was had a flashlight. The beam was too concentrated to be a lantern.

Just then a contraction hit her. She gasped and bit her lip, working to stay quiet.

Deke? Where are you?

The footsteps grew louder and the flashlight's beam flitted across the alcove's entrance.

Her breath caught. Had they missed it?

It snapped back.

Her mouth went dry. She drew her feet up, trying to make herself as small as possible while the flashlight penetrated the darkness in front of her.

Then the pale blue moonlight was blocked by shadows—two shadows, and the beam swept back and forth, back and forth, as it crawled toward her along the dirt floor.

It touched the toes of her shoes. The sensation was almost physical.

She couldn't get a breath. Her left hand instinctively cradled her tummy as the circle of light climbed up her leg.

It was almost a relief when the beam finally blinded her.

"Hello, Mrs. Cunningham." The voice was unmistakable. Frank James. "Shame on your husband for leaving you alone."

AN HOUR LATER, HE FELT cool air on his heated face. In the next instant, his eyes detected a difference in the total blackness before him.

It was the end of the tunnel. He slowed, using his instincts and his honed senses to assess any danger, before he burst out into the open.

What if Novus had blown those tunnels, not because he didn't have enough men, but to separate Deke and Mindy? If he guessed that Deke would leave Mindy to investigate the explosions, this would be the perfect time to have James capture her.

Flattening himself against the tunnel opening, he scanned the open area.

Nothing.

As much as he wanted to believe that nothing was a good thing, his natural caution told him otherwise. He longed to rush over to the alcove and take Mindy into his arms, but he had to proceed as if he were infiltrating enemy lines.

Sweat trickled down the side of his face. He wiped it away, and felt the heat radiating from his skin.

He had a fever. That meant his damn arm was infected. He laid his palm on the bandage covering his wound. Sure enough, it was hot, too. And the pressure of his hand was excruciating.

Judging by the way his head kept threatening to spin and by the blackness encroaching on his vision, he was close to passing out. He swallowed.

Damn close.

He took a deep breath and eased out into the open. Hugging the wall, he slid around to the edge of the alcove, scanning the room the whole time, alert to any slight movement or sound.

He set the lantern down and lit it awkwardly. He held it in his right hand and brandished the crowbar in his left.

His pulse drummed in his ears and his heartbeat shot sky-high. He wished it was merely the anticipation of seeing Mindy safe and sound, but he knew it was an adrenaline response, readying him to attack.

Rocking to the balls of his feet, he angled around the alcove opening.

No Mindy. Even though he'd expected it, his heart sank. She wasn't where he'd left her.

At that moment, a movement in the shadows at the back caught his eye.

"Mindy?" Even as the word formed on his lips, the shadow lunged toward him. Mindy couldn't stand up by herself, much less lunge.

He swung the crowbar with all his might, following it with the lantern. The arc of flame revealed a glimpse of a grimacing black mask of a face with bared teeth gleaming.

Then a huge weight sent him plummeting backward. His skull slammed into the dirt floor—hard. Pain blinded him. A dreadful growling filled his ears.

He tried to roll away, but the monster rolled with him, trailed by a strange orange light. He blinked. It was a man—a very big black man with his hair on fire.

The man shook his head, flinging drops of hot oil onto Deke's face, and propelled himself toward the spring. He dunked his head, frantically trying to douse the flames.

Deke retrieved his crowbar and followed him. Awkwardly, he gripped the crowbar, wishing he was left-handed, and drew his arm back.

When the man lifted his head, Deke leaped, swinging. The crowbar connected with a loud crack.

The man dropped like a stone, and Deke's momentum carried him right over him. He landed sideways on his injured arm. He clamped his jaw and hissed.

Breathing hard, he got his feet under him and crouched over the unconscious man. He patted him down and hit pay dirt. A portable Taser—dripping wet.

Deke grabbed it. Just looking at it tightened his muscles in involuntary reaction. He shook it and dried it on his pants, then examined it. He started to turn it on, but on second though he decided to give it time to dry out.

Pocketing it, he dropped to his haunches. He needed a couple of minutes to rest before he headed back toward the hotel.

After a few deep breaths and a swallow of water, he headed across the spring. He eyed the tunnels for a moment, then turned and looked at the rusted car that held the dynamite.

A sense of inevitability settled on his shoulders. As dangerous as it was, he had to carry the old, unstable explosive back to the hotel. He had to blow the two remaining entrances to the mine. He couldn't take the chance that James might escape through them, or force Mindy back into this dark abyss.

He swayed and had to steady himself against the wall. He clenched his teeth, refusing to give in to the fever that was trying to take him down. He couldn't. He had to keep going.

This time, if he failed, Mindy would die, and so would his son.

Chapter Nine

The pitch-black tunnel seemed endless. Deke trudged along, carefully balancing the dynamite and blasting caps in the crude sling he'd made from the musty blanket, and using the crowbar as a walking stick. It was a sobering thought that he was carrying his own mode of destruction. He was literally a walking, ticking bomb.

But the dynamite wasn't his biggest worry. His biggest worry was that he wouldn't make it. He was having a hard time putting one foot in front of the other. And he felt cold and hot at the same time.

In a part of his brain he was trying to ignore, he knew what was wrong. His arm was bleeding again. The knife wound ached with a stomach-churning pain that turned the edge of his vision black. When he'd looked at it, he'd seen the red line running up his arm. It was an artery, and it was infected. If that line got much closer to his heart, he'd be in real danger of dying.

He'd tried Mindy's home remedy for stanching the bleeding. He'd gathered up spiderwebs and pressed them into the oozing gash on his arm. Then he'd rebandaged it. Not surprisingly, they'd helped for a while.

And if he'd been able to immobilize his arm, they probably would have stopped the bleeding entirely, just like Mindy had said they would.

He'd stopped trying to use his arm, working hard to keep it still. He'd draped it over the dynamite-filled blanket, and occasionally he felt the faint tickle of a drop of blood running down his wrist to drip slowly off his fingers.

He stumbled over a rock, catching himself just in time, cringing as he had to adjust the blanket containing the dynamite. The misstep jarred his arm and turned the darkness in front of his eyes into a bright fireworks show. He ducked his head and braced himself against the wall. He needed to shut his eyes for just a few moments, until the fireworks went away.

WHEN HE OPENED HIS EYES AGAIN, he was crouched against the wall. He'd fallen asleep—or passed out, for no telling how long. At least the blanket was still in place, slung over his shoulder.

Breathing through his mouth, trying to settle his racing heart, he lifted his head and blinked.

Was he still woozy, or was that a real light in front of him? It didn't dance around, and it wasn't the same bright yellow as his internal fireworks show.

This light was dim and pale and vaguely rectangular. A lump of relief closed the back of his throat and stung his eyes.

It was the end of the tunnel. Where Mindy was. Just a few yards farther. He covered half the remaining distance before he had to stop.

He pressed his back to the wall and rested his head against it for a moment. With his eyes closed, he pictured the small anteroom that connected the tunnels with the hotel basement. He'd returned the way he'd gone, back through the south tunnel—had it just been yesterday?

He was less than two yards from the anteroom. He had to work fast. He carefully placed the blanket-covered dynamite on the floor just inside the tunnel entrance. He'd already attached one of the blasting caps and a length of fuse to the sticks. So all he had to do was unroll the fuse and light it.

He started working, but he kept losing focus. What the hell was the matter with him? His legs were heavy and slow. Sweat rolled down his face, chilling his skin. He shuddered and concentrated on making it to the south wall. He slid along it, keeping to the shadows until he reached the framed doorway. Then he stopped and listened.

Nothing.

To the east was the trapdoor, and on the north wall was the massive wooden door through which James had disappeared.

Before he positioned the fuse, he had something he wanted to check out. After listening again and hearing nothing, he moved from the dirt wall to the timbers that framed the tunnel opening. He angled around quickly, sweeping the room quickly with his gaze, then ducked back behind the timbers.

He looked at the trapdoor through which he'd crawled earlier. He'd discarded it because Mindy would never be able to crawl through the small opening.

But the thing that had puzzled him ever since he first knocked on that wood still held his interest. Sixty years ago, this alcove had obviously provided a passage from the hotel and the building to the north into the mine from the two buildings. That trapdoor must have once been a full-size doorway.

Deke gripped the crowbar in his hand and examined the wooden planks carefully. Whereas the other side looked like a door, this side appeared to be a rough-hewn planked wall, except that the planks above the trapdoor looked newer than the rest.

There *was* a door there. Relief stung his throat and turned the back of his neck clammy. With the noise he was about to make, he figured he had two minutes at the most before one of James's men saw or heard him.

He attached the fuse to the dynamite and ran it along the wall to the north door. There was barely enough to reach. He didn't know much about detonation. That was Brock's specialty. But he knew that fuse burned rapidly, so he figured he had about enough to last five minutes.

Five minutes to get Mindy outside to safety. If she was in there. Through the haze in his brain, Deke tried to remember why he was sure that was where Frank was holding her. He couldn't. But it hardly mattered. It could be their only chance.

He set the end of the fuse down at the edge of the inner door, praying he'd be able to come back and light it. He patted his jeans pocket, where the disposable lighter was.

That much dynamite would blow this whole basement area to smithereens, if the fuse stayed lit.

Then he turned to the door. He had maybe three minutes before the noise of prying the planks away from the door alerted James.

Here goes. He started with the planks at knee level,

just above the top of the trapdoor. The nails screeched and the wood creaked. But within thirty seconds he had two of the twelve-inch-wide planks off and had started on a third.

Sure enough, the wood behind the cross-nailed planks was just like the wood he'd kicked in to get through the trapdoor. He figured with one or two well-placed kicks he could have an opening that was thirty inches wide and about three and a half to four feet tall. Plenty of room for Mindy to get through. If he had the strength to kick the boards away.

By the time the third plank let go, he was reeling from exhaustion. Fever from loss of blood, he was sure. He gulped in a lungful of air, hoping it would fortify him for another few seconds. He reared back and kicked the door. Wood splintered loudly.

At that moment, the north door opened and two soldiers in desert camo grabbed him, jerking the crowbar out of his hands and wrenching his arms behind his back. He groaned out loud at the screaming pain in his right arm.

Somehow, the pain heightened his senses. Suddenly, he was hyperaware of everything around him. The bright light from the open door. The air that swirled about him, evaporating the sweat and cooling his skin. The loud, sawing breathing of the two guards.

They shoved him through the door into a narrow foyer. He directed all his strength toward staying aware of everything around him. There were three doors in the tiny foyer. Besides the one they'd pushed him through, there was a door to his left and one directly in front of him. He was about to find out where at least one of those doors led.

A guard pushed open the door in front of him.

Across a short expanse of rough flooring, lit by a single bare bulb, he saw Mindy. Tied up and gagged.

His heart slammed against his chest with a ferocity that left him breathless.

"Mindy," he rasped. His throat closed up and his eyes stung with relief. He hadn't let himself even think of the possibility that she wasn't behind the door. But now, seeing her, he knew he'd feared just that.

She shook her head violently. He nodded slightly, hoping to send her the message that he knew James was waiting for him. That he was prepared.

By the look in her wide, frightened eyes he knew he wasn't fooling her. With one quick glance, she saw how sick he was. How weak.

She knew that he wasn't prepared. That he wasn't even sure how much longer he could stay upright.

Her gaze dropped to his right hand and back to meet his eyes. She knew how long it had been since James had cut his arm. He could see in her eyes that she was calculating the amount of blood he'd lost and how far along the infection was. She shook her head again.

He sent her what he hoped was an encouraging smile and took a step forward.

With a *whoosh* of noise, spotlights flared, blinding him. Immediately, the sound of weapons being raised hit his ears. And slowly, as the red spots from the lights faded, the outlines of three men coalesced. They were dressed in military fatigues and boots, and were aiming their weapons at his head.

The smallest man slung his rifle over his shoulder and stepped over to Mindy's side. He extracted a 9 mm handgun from a side holster and pointed it at the side of her head.

"Nice of you to join us. What were you doing out there, tearing through the wall? Trying to get away and leave your pretty girl behind? That's cold."

Deke's gaze snapped to the speaker. The accompanying movement of his head made the edges of his vision turn dark again.

Still, there was no mistaking who the speaker was. It was Frank James—without his bandanna. No question. As he thought, the face was so close to the sketch of Novus as to almost be identical.

Deke blinked to clear his vision and studied James's face. Somehow, without the bandanna covering his lower face, his eyes seemed more pronounced.

And familiar.

"Hey, Min. You feeling better?" he said casually, inwardly wincing at the sound of his voice. It wouldn't fool an infant, much less a roomful of trained combatants.

Mindy nodded, but her face was still drawn and pale, and she looked exhausted. Worse, if he could judge by the look in her eyes, she was worried about *him.*

"She's doing just fine, Cunningham. When we found her where you'd abandoned her, she was in a lot of pain. But thanks to some friends of ours, we were able to figure out what was wrong and correct it."

Correct it? Bile churned in Deke's stomach. "I swear to God," he said hoarsely, "if you hurt her, or—"

"Calm down, Cunningham. The drug we gave her is a medication that's commonly used for preterm labor. Ask your wife."

"You've got a gun to her head. What do you think she's going to say?" He met Mindy's gaze, and saw that James was telling the truth. *If* he could still read her as well as he once could.

"You'll see that she's no longer in labor. And she's feeling fine, which is more than I can say for you right now."

Deke shook his head and concentrated on the pip-squeak's words. He was well aware of the blood slowly oozing out of his wounded arm, and the clammy sweat prickling his forehead and neck. It infuriated him that he was letting a little knife wound affect him.

"Don't worry about me," he growled.

"I'm not. Trust me." James grinned, and the thing that had been bothering Deke ever since the first time he'd seen the fake cowboy suddenly came clear.

Of course Frank James was Novus Ordo's brother. But looking at him, Deke realized something else. Those eyes had looked at him from behind the shemagh every day while he was held prisoner by Novus.

It was Novus himself who'd held the gun to Deke's head, who'd grinned at him when he'd ordered him to rise to his knees. His eyes were older and more sinister than James's, but they were the same eyes.

James nodded his head. The three guards stepped toward Deke in unison, their weapons still raised.

Deke noticed that they were—to a man—Middle Eastern in appearance. Novus's men who'd infiltrated the United States. A chill ran through him. The implications were ominous.

On a few days' notice, Novus Ordo had brought together a half dozen armed and trained zealots to carry out a plan he was creating on the fly.

At least a half dozen. Probably more.

"What do you want from me, James?"

"Okay, Cunningham. Time to do a little business."

"You've heard my offer. It hasn't changed."

"Sure. I know your offer. I let your wife—'scuse me, *ex*-wife—go, and you'll answer all my questions. And I'm sure you're telling the truth—you'll answer my questions. But all your answers will be lies." He shook his head, laughing. "Now I'm sure that you've practiced 'em until they sound just as good as the truth—even while you're being tortured."

"Nnh," Mindy moaned and struggled, and shook her head. "Nnnh—nhh."

He knew exactly what she was saying. *Tell them.* He loved her for caring whether they hurt him. But there was far more at stake here than the lives of two people.

"I'll tell you the truth," he said quietly.

Mindy couldn't take her eyes off Deke. She was so glad he was here. And so worried about him.

Spots of color stained his cheeks, standing out against his pale skin and pinched mouth. His right hand hung useless at his side, and a drop of blood shimmered on the end of one finger. Also, one end of the bandage she'd made out of his shirt dangled from the sleeve of his shearling jacket. It, too, looked soaked with blood.

Mindy's stomach churned. It had been doing flip-flops ever since the nurse had given her the injection of magnesium sulfate.

Deke must have lost at least a pint of blood, maybe more. She wondered how long the wound had been actively bleeding. She'd wrapped it as well as she could, but she'd known it would eventually come loose and separate the edges of the cut. She'd intended to be there to rewrap it.

No, truthfully, she'd hoped they would be out of here safe and sound by now, and he'd have a stitched-up arm and a course of antibiotics for the infection.

Acrid saliva filled her mouth. She swallowed and focused all her strength on not giving in to the nausea. Magnesium sulfate was excellent for slowing premature labor, but it was also excellent for causing nausea. She clenched her teeth against the queasiness, praying that she wouldn't throw up while her mouth was gagged.

At least these terrorists had a health professional in their group. Although the idea that they had soldiers and nurses and God only knew who else available inside the United States was a sobering one.

"Just let Mindy go," Deke muttered. His words sounded slurred.

Frank James laughed.

As calmly as she could, Mindy assessed their situation. Not good.

Judging by the lack of color in his face and the way he was swaying, it was a miracle that he was still upright.

A miracle and a testament to his strength of will and his determination. He needed lots of fluids, and probably a blood transfusion.

His skin looked tight and drawn across his cheekbones. His mouth was compressed into a thin line, and his nostrils and the corners of his lips were white and pinched. Sweat glistened on his forehead and neck.

Stay with me, Deke. Don't quit now, she wanted to say. But that wasn't fair. He was the strongest man she'd ever met. He would die for an innocent. She knew he'd endure anything for his son. But he'd pushed himself further than any normal human being could have. He'd pushed himself past his body's limits, and it was shutting down.

The idea that he was mortal, that there was a point beyond which even his steely resolve couldn't push, sent a soul-deep terror searing through her like a spark touching a line of gasoline. The terror manifested itself physically as paralyzing nausea.

Her throat was too dry to swallow, so she squeezed her eyes shut and waited until the red haze of intense queasiness passed.

At that instant, Sprout kicked her, as if to remind her that everything she did, everything she felt, affected him, too.

For the moment, the mag sulfate had done its job. But every few moments, she felt little aftershocks of contractions.

At eight-plus months, Sprout was capable of surviving on his own. With her knowledge and experience, she'd bet money that Deke's son would be born within the next twenty-four hours.

She did not want him born in an underground mine, held hostage by terrorists. And she certainly did not want him born an orphan.

She had to come up with a plan.

"You sound sincere, Cunningham. But then you always do. Even with a gun at *your* head, you still lie."

The gun barrel pressed against Mindy's head dug into her flesh. She couldn't see James, but she could see Deke.

His pallor had taken on a gray tinge, and his eyes weren't focused on anything. He took a stumbling step forward.

A soldier stepped in front of him and swung the butt of his gun at his head. The impact sounded like a gunshot.

Deke slumped to the ground.

"No!" Mindy screamed through her gag.

"Get up!" the guard growled in a heavy accent. He raised the gun butt again.

"Stop!" she cried desperately.

"Hold it," James snapped. "Careful. He's no good to us dead. Pull his head up. I want him to see this."

The guard grabbed a handful of Deke's hair and jerked his head up.

Deke rose to his knees, swaying. He squeezed his eyes shut, then blinked several times. The guard's blow hadn't broken the skin, but he was going to have a black eye and one hell of a headache.

Don't fight them, she begged silently.

"Let's see if you can lie while there's a gun at your wife's head. Is it loaded? Is it not?" He cocked the hammer of the .45. Mindy closed her eyes.

"What do you think, Mrs. Cunningham?" He jerked the bandanna away from her mouth.

She winced, and felt Sprout move in reaction to her pain. She licked her dry, chapped lips.

He wasn't going to kill her. He couldn't. If James killed her, he'd never get anything out of Deke. Somehow, her argument didn't make her feel better, considering the gun barrel pressed to her temple.

Deke's jaw clenched and his chin ratcheted up a notch. His face was pale as death. "Wait—" he muttered.

"Deke, no," she gasped. "He won't do it. He needs me."

"You think so?" James mumbled, easing the pressure of the barrel against her temple.

Mindy held her breath.

"I don't know whether Rook is alive—"

James pushed the gun's barrel against her head again.

"I don't know," Deke said quickly, "but I know the most likely place he'd be."

"You know where he might be if he were alive, which you don't know." James barked a short derisive laugh. "Sorry, I just don't buy it. You're not quite ready to tell the truth." He squeezed the trigger, and the hammer clicked—a hollow sound that seemed to hover in the air.

Mindy's chest was tight with tension. She struggled for breath, as Sprout moved restlessly inside her. Fine tremors rippled through her limbs.

James made a gesture that she could barely see out of the corner of her eye. Two guards rushed toward Deke and jerked him upright. He didn't speak. Mindy had no idea if it was stoicism or pain and exhaustion.

His head lolled on his neck. He could hardly stand on his own.

"All right, Cunningham. Let's see how much stamina you've got. Every hour on the hour I'm gonna stick one live round into this gun, spin the chamber and put it against your wife's head and—bam!" He grinned. "Or not. Every hour on the half hour, I'm gonna break one of your fingers. So don't count on being able to handle a weapon." He nodded to the guards.

The two men pulled Deke to his feet and began to half drag him to a door in the back of the room.

"By the way, Cunningham. There's only one thing we want to know. You lead us to Castle, and we'll make sure your wife and baby are safe."

Deke muttered a curse aimed at James.

The fake cowboy just chuckled.

Mindy hoped that in his dazed and injured state, Deke knew what she knew.

Frank James had shown his face to them. There was no way he was going to let them live.

Chapter Ten

There was a clock on the wall, put there on purpose, Mindy was sure, so she could watch the minute hand go around. So she could anticipate, minute by minute, second by second, the instant when the guards would break one of Deke's fingers.

Then she'd have to watch the crawling hand for another half hour as she waited for James to come in, stand in front of her and load the single bullet into the revolver. Then he'd spin the chamber, press the barrel to her head and pull the trigger.

A twinge—like a miniature contraction, tightened her abdominal muscles for an instant.

Settle down, Sprout. You stay put. Mommy needs time to figure out a way to save your daddy.

There had to be a trick to it. Didn't there? As long as Novus believed Deke had the information he needed, he wouldn't kill her. Nor would he leave her life or death—or anything else he could control—to chance. So the bullet in the spinning chamber had to be a fake.

The minute hand bumped forward. Her heart bumped against her chest. It was eleven twenty-nine. One minute until they broke Deke's finger.

She opened her mouth and screamed. She didn't know why James had removed the gag, but she was thankful that he had.

"Don't do it!" she yelled. "Stop! I'll make him talk! I swear! Just don't hurt him!"

She stopped, holding her breath, but the only thing she heard was the silence.

"Don't hurt him!" Her eyes were glued to the clock.

The minute hand quivered.

"Please!" she whispered in desperation, as tears welled in her eyes.

It jerked forward. And centered on the six.

"No!" she screamed as the tears streamed down her face. "No! Please!"

The door behind her opened.

She twisted, straining to see who'd entered the room. "Who is it? Is that you, James?"

The man who called himself Frank James stepped into her field of vision. "What are you yelling about?" he asked in an impatient tone.

"Where's Deke? Is he all right? Did you—"

James held up his hand. "Slow down. Try to stay calm. Now what are you saying?"

Mindy glared at the man who held Deke's well-being and the fate of her child in his hands. "Please bring Deke back in here, or take me to him. I'll make him tell you the truth."

James assessed her. "Has he told you the truth?"

She did her best not to look away from his staring eyes, but she couldn't stop herself from blinking.

"So he has. Well, the truth is the truth, no matter who delivers it. Why don't you tell me what he told you?"

She dropped her gaze then, wondering what Deke would want her to say.

He took a step toward her. "Mrs. Cunningham?"

"He told me he doesn't know where Rook is." She looked up at the fake cowboy.

James's beady eyes studied her face for a long moment. She could see the little wheels in his little brain turning, and hear what he was thinking. He had to decide if he believed her.

She tried to keep her expression bland, even as her mind raced. Ever since James had captured her she'd known this moment would come. But she still hadn't figured out what she was going to tell him.

She knew one thing though. If she admitted to James that Deke had no idea where Rook was, then James would come to the same conclusion she had. *They'd be of no more use to him.*

Finally he spoke. "Do you believe him?"

Slowly, deliberately, she met Frank James's gaze. "No," she said.

James's eyes twinkled and his mouth twitched. For the life of her Mindy couldn't figure out if he was amused by her or pleased that he'd gotten her to tell the truth.

"Why should I believe you?"

"Men care about country. About honor. About freedom. They will die for any of those things." She took a long breath. "But I'm a woman. There are only two things I would die for," she said evenly, as she cradled her stomach. "My child and Deke. And I don't want to die."

James laughed. "Well said, Mrs. Cunningham."

"So you'll bring Deke to me?"

"I'll let you know." James turned and left through the door.

"Wait!" she cried. "You're underestimating me. I can make him tell. Please wait!"

But the door closed with an unmistakable finality. James wasn't coming back. Not anytime soon.

DEKE RAISED HIS HEAD, wondering if he'd been asleep or if he'd passed out. Either way, his head felt heavy and swollen, and his eyes stung with the clammy sweat that poured off his forehead.

For a couple of seconds, he wasn't sure where he was. He tried to lift a hand to wipe his face, and found out he couldn't. He was tied up—again.

The memories came back. He and Mindy were prisoners of a ridiculous costumed cowboy who called himself Frank James, and who so far hadn't admitted that he was working for Novus Ordo. He was, though. Deke was sure of it.

He almost laughed. Were these knots going to be as easy to undo as the others were? Not a chance. As weak and sick as he felt, he wouldn't be able to untie a birthday bow.

He was sitting in a hard wooden chair behind a desk. He looked down and saw that his left hand was tied to the chair's arm.

He glanced at his right hand, which was lashed to the opposite chair arm. It was red with blood from the slash on his forearm. He stared at the bandaged wound.

How had that happened? He had a vague recollection of a hand slashing through the air and burning pain, but that was all. No face. No name.

He did remember the bandage. It was his shirt—a

brand-new white dress shirt. Mindy had torn it apart to fashion the makeshift bandage.

It had served fairly well. The material still partially covered the wound, but here and there, where the blood-soaked strips had slipped, he could see the jagged, inflamed edges of the wound.

He blinked, trying to clear the stinging sweat from his eyes, and noticed that his fingers were moving. Was he doing that? He really didn't know.

He looked up, seeking the source of light in the room. It was a lamp, with only one bare bulb in it, sitting on the scarred wooden desk. It provided very little light—just enough for him to make out what was around him.

The big desk, of course, which sat directly across the room from the door. And the lamp, an old-fashioned leather desk blotter that held a 1959 calendar from Sundance Printing Company, and a pen stand with a wooden fountain pen. There were several ink stains on the polished surface of the desk.

Heavy, dark curtains covered the windows behind him, so he assumed he was aboveground. Probably the mine foreman's office, or maybe the office of the hotel manager.

On either side of the door were ancient, dusty barrister bookcases stuffed full of old books, folders and stacks of paper. Mindy would have a fit. She loved old books.

His mouth turned up in a wry smile. Mindy. He'd have to tell her about the bookcases, once they were safe.

All at once, the significance of those last words hit him. *Once they were safe.* That meant they weren't—Mindy wasn't.

Now he remembered, and all his scattered thoughts began to coalesce. He'd come here to rescue Mindy. They'd been trapped in an abandoned mine, and Frank James had cut him with his own knife.

More memories assaulted his brain. He'd gone looking for a way out of the mine, but he'd run into a cave-in. Then when he got back to where he'd left Mindy, she was gone, captured again by Frank James.

The sound of the hammer clicking against metal rang in his ears. The sound of one more day.

No. Not one more day. One more *hour.*

He didn't have a day because within a few minutes someone was going to walk in here with a heavy hammer and smash one of his fingers.

Then a half hour after that, they were going to play Russian roulette with Mindy again.

He wished he knew how long he'd been here. If he hadn't passed out, maybe he could have figured out a plan to get out of here and save Mindy.

Mindy didn't deserve any of this. She was innocent. As innocent as a newborn baby.

Baby. Deke blinked slowly and felt himself drifting off to sleep again.

If he could just wipe his eyes. They stung and itched like fire, until he couldn't think of anything else.

He lifted his hand and rediscovered that it wouldn't lift. He wiggled his fingers, idly wondering which one they'd break first. He shuddered with anticipated pain.

It hardly mattered. He just wished they'd come and get it over with. Then he could stop worrying about it and think about rescuing Mindy.

He drummed his fingers, one at a time, on the wooden desk and sleepily chanted, "One, two, three four five. Once I caught a fish alive." He started over. "Six, seven, eight nine ten. Then I let him go again. One, two—"

He heard something and froze, with his third, fourth and fifth fingers in the air.

He didn't move for a long time, but nothing else happened. It must have been the wooden beams creaking, or a clod of dirt falling.

One, two, three four five—

He shook his head. He had to get that annoying nursery rhyme out of his head.

Maybe he should search the room for hidden cameras. He wasn't sure what good finding them would do him, but at least he'd be doing something, rather than drifting off into unconsciousness.

While they were in the air force, Matt Parker had developed a foolproof visual search grid for assessing the danger points in a specified terrain. Maybe he could use the same principle to search this room for a camera.

He quelled the voice in his head that kept trying to chant the nursery rhyme and concentrated on the grid. He was almost done when he heard the doorknob rattle.

The wooden door swung open with a loud creak.

It was Frank James. And one of the soldiers was with him. The soldier held a hammer.

"Here we are, Cunningham. Ready to make good on our promise." James grinned, showing crooked teeth. "Got anything to say? Or should we just get to it."

"By all means, go ahead," Deke said hoarsely. "I've got nothing to say."

James nodded at the other man, who stepped up to the chair. He was holding a small sledgehammer—

probably six pounds. Enough to make mush out of his fingers.

The soldier took a balanced stance, then reared back like a baseball player, holding the hammer in both hands, and prepared to swing.

Deke wanted more than anything in the world to look James in the eye as the hammer came down on his hand, but he couldn't stop himself from cringing.

He closed his eyes and clenched his jaw so he wouldn't scream.

"Wait!"

Deke jerked at the single explosive word. Sweat rolled off his forehead and into his eyes.

James had stopped the soldier.

A painful spasm of reaction shrieked through his arm, from the shoulder all the way down to his fingers.

"Sorry about that, Cunningham, I almost forgot something." James smiled. "How would you like to see your wife?"

Deke swallowed bile and opened his eyes to a slit. "What are you talking about?" he asked, his stomach churning with worry. What was James up to now?

"I'm asking you a simple question. Your wife begged me not to break your fingers. Begged me to let her see you. She said she had something to say to you."

There was no way Deke was going to trust James. "What did you do to her?" He sat up as straight as he could and clenched his teeth against the dizziness that threatened to spin his head right off.

"Do to her? Me? Nothing. I told you my plan. You know exactly what I planned to do. But Mrs. Cunningham is so sweet and lovely, I couldn't deny her request."

"Great. I want to see her, too." Deke spoke in a toneless, measured voice. He wasn't sure what James was up to, but whatever it was, he knew it was designed to get him to waver.

And it had probably been planned by Novus.

Rather than ask James more questions, Deke closed his eyes. "I'm not feeling too good, so whatever you've got planned, can you hurry up? I'm pretty sure I'm in danger of bleeding to death, and I would definitely like to see my wife before I die."

"Your ex-wife," James corrected him. He nodded at the soldier who set the sledgehammer down and left the room.

"I've got a message for you to give Novus," Deke said, as soon as the man left.

James waved a hand dismissively. "I have no idea what you're talking about, but fine. Give me the message. I'm sure it'll be funny."

"You tell Novus Ordo he made a mistake when he targeted my friends and my wife. He's dealt with me before and he knows I mean what I say. Tell him if it's the last thing I do on this earth, I'm coming to get him."

James chuckled. "That is funny. You're talking about Novus Ordo, the international terrorist? That's some imagination you've got."

James bent down until he was mere inches away from Deke's face. "Now let me give you a message. You think you're so smart? You don't know anything. Treating me like I'm nobody? You'll soon find out just who I am, and when you do, I'm going to be right here, in your face. And I'll make you sorry you didn't respect me."

Through the haze that kept drifting in front of his

eyes, Deke stared at James's thin, weaselly face and dark, beady eyes.

He closed his eyes, trying to give James the impression that he was totally bored with his threat while he drew on his memory, conjuring up the likeness of Novus Ordo that Rook had described to the facial recognition artist for the CIA.

James had to be related to Novus. Deke could believe he *was* Novus, except that Novus was too smart to place himself smack in the middle of a terrorist plot in the U.S.

He squeezed his eyes shut tighter, and a splash of reddish stars appeared before his closed eyelids. He squinted open one eye and saw that James had straightened and was watching him with a vicious hatred.

He drew a deep breath, then another, trying to ward off the loss of consciousness with an overload of oxygen. It helped a little.

The doorknob turned, and the soldier was back with Mindy in tow. Her hands were still tied behind her back.

When she saw Deke, her face turned white and she swayed. The soldier tightened his hold on her arm.

"Deke. Did he—?" Her eyes flew to his bound hands, then to his face. As soon as she looked into his eyes, she relaxed. "Oh, thank God."

James gestured to a straight-backed chair on the other side of the desk. "Here you are, Mrs. Cunningham."

"For heaven's sake, give my husband some water," Mindy cried. "He's about to pass out. He's lost too much blood. He needs fluids. Where's that nurse of yours?"

James nodded at the soldier, who turned and left the room.

"Are you okay?" Deke asked her.

"For now," she said. "The medication they gave me did stop the contractions, at least so far."

The man dressed in desert camo was back almost immediately with a big jar of water. James took it from him and held it to Deke's lips. He wasn't careful, and a lot of the liquid spilled down Deke's bare chest and torso, but Deke managed to gulp down at least a pint's worth.

He did feel better immediately. It washed the haze from his brain and the heaviness from his eyelids and limbs.

"Now that we've provided *room service,* take her and tie her to that straight-backed chair," James instructed his sidekick.

"Please don't," she begged him. "I'm so sick. If the contractions start again, I'll need to lie down. Tie my hands in front of me, but please don't tie me to that chair. If I go into labor, I have to be able to move or—" Her eyes filled with tears. "Or," she sobbed. "I'm going to lose my baby."

James rolled his eyes. "Fine. You'll have your hands tied in front and you won't be tied down. So let me save you some trouble, Mrs. Cunningham. There's no need for you to go exploring around the room. It's been completely cleaned out. There's nothing in here you can use as a weapon. Nothing that you can cut your ropes with. I'd hate for anything to happen to your kid. I've only got so much patience. If you or Cunningham try anything, I'll go back to my original plan—with one change."

He looked at Deke, then at her. "Instead of breaking his fingers, I think I'll just go ahead and cut 'em off. I've got a cigar cutter that ought to do the trick just fine."

Mindy swayed. Only the man's hand on her arm kept her from falling.

"For God's sake, James. What did you bring her here for? There's no reason she has to go through this."

"I'll let her tell you why she's here." He turned to his sidekick. "Tie her hands in front of her."

"Not tie to the chair?" the man asked in broken English.

"No." James half turned toward the door. "Goodbye, Mrs. Cunningham. I'll be looking forward to talking with you. I'll see both of you in one hour."

The door closed quietly behind them as they left.

Mindy opened her mouth to speak, but Deke shook his head.

"Wait," he mouthed.

She nodded.

Deke waited a full five minutes—probably more. He counted to sixty five times, then added another sixty for a buffer, in case he'd counted too fast.

Meeting Mindy's gaze, he motioned with his head for her to come over to his chair.

She slowly pushed herself up out of the straight-backed chair and walked over to stand in front of him.

"Lean down," he whispered.

As soon as he smelled her tangerine scent and felt her hair soft and tickly against his lips, he whispered, "I've grid-searched the room. I'm pretty sure there are no cameras, but there could be recording devices. So play along with the things I say out loud, and whisper to answer my whispers. Do you still have the knife?"

She nodded, pointing to her breasts where she'd hidden it before.

"Good girl." Then he said aloud, "Why did James say he'd let you tell me why he brought you here?"

"Deke, please," Mindy answered, as she worked to retrieve the knife with her bound hands. "I was so worried about you. I was afraid they'd broken your fingers. Tell him what he wants to know. He'll let us go."

She finally had the knife in her hands. She pushed the button that snicked the blade into place.

Deke indicated his hands with a nod. "I *was* telling the truth. Are you saying you don't believe me?"

Mindy quickly cut the ropes binding his hands to the chair. He flexed his left hand, then his right.

"How can I believe you? You've lied to me over and over again." Mindy's eyes filled with tears and she shook her head.

Deke knew she was apologizing for saying those things to him, but he also knew he deserved them. He hadn't lied overtly to her, but he'd lied by omission, time and time again.

"I'm sorry, Min. I never meant to hurt you."

She blinked and the tears fell down her cheeks.

Taking the knife, he slipped it between her hands and cut the ropes binding her.

"Deke, tell me what you know. I know you haven't been truthful with James. Why would you, after what he's done to us?"

"You think I know something about Rook? Hell, Mindy. He was my best friend, and Novus had him killed. Even if I did know anything, I wouldn't tell that slimy terrorist."

She leaned closer. "What now?" she whispered.

"Do you know what time it is?" he whispered back to her.

She looked at him in surprise. "About three-thirty. Why?"

He shook his head. He wasn't about to tell her what he had planned. "And today is Saturday?"

She nodded in answer. "But Deke," she said out loud, "if Novus had Rook killed, why is he doing this? Why does he think Rook might still be alive?"

"The same reason Irina couldn't give up. Because they never recovered a body. Novus must not trust his sniper's aim. Besides, don't you think if Rook were still alive, he'd have contacted Irina? Do you think he'd have let her believe he was dead all this time?"

Mindy stared at Deke. She'd never thought about that before. What if Rook were alive? "He could have been horribly wounded and didn't want her to see him. Or maybe he has amnesia."

Deke frowned at her, but made a sound like a laugh. "All right, Mindy. Back off the romancing."

But her brain was racing. If Novus's man had killed Rook, wouldn't he have known it? Wouldn't the body have surfaced eventually? "Maybe Rook *is* hiding. Maybe he's alive, but he wants Novus to think he's dead. Maybe he's out there searching for Novus."

Deke pulled his right arm into his side and sent a scowl her way. "What was in that medicine they gave you? You're getting ridiculous. Rook is dead, and Novus holding a gun to my head or yours isn't going to change that."

Chapter Eleven

"Okay, it's done. I've worked out a way to get past security and into the house. It's going to be very tricky, though, so we probably ought to use it as a last resort."

"Last resort? What good is a last resort if we don't have a first *resort?"*

"That's just it. I'm working on something else. It'll be much cleaner and less risky. Tomorrow is Irina's regular monthly visit to the Children's Burn Center. She never misses going when she's in town. She'll probably get one of the specialists to drive her. I'm sure that's how Cunningham told her to handle it."

"So what's your big plan?"

"Shoot the specialist—wound him—just enough to put him in the hospital for a day or two. That buys us another couple of days. If one of her employees is in the hospital, she'll be there every day."

"That's your big plan? There are holes big enough to drive a semitrailer through."

"Yeah? You have a better idea?"

The voice on the other end of the line was silent for a few seconds. "You think I've got sharpshooters sitting around waiting for something to do? Keep working on a way to get past security. That spread is huge. There's got to be a few feet that are undefended."

"What about Cunningham?"

The man on the phone cursed in Arabic. "He's still swearing that Rook is dead. Even when he's alone with his wife."

"You think Cunningham doesn't suspect that you have every corner of every room bugged? Stop fooling with them. Stop just threatening the wife. Do some real damage."

A frustrated growl echoed through the phone. "I'm not sure Elliott has the stomach for that."

He sympathized with the man on the phone. He understood family loyalty, too, all too well. But it was sounding more and more like Elliott was a coward.

"Maybe you should have somebody in there that does *have the stomach."*

Sudden silence crackled across the miles. He sat there, watching his hand shake. Had he gone too far? He'd just given one of the most dangerous men on the planet a surefire plan to assassinate him—or one of his teammates.

"You just deliver Irina Castle to me. I'll take care of Cunningham."

"Don't make the mistake of underestimating him. Whatever else he is, I can guarantee you he's not stupid."

"WHAT ARE WE GOING TO DO, Deke?" Mindy whispered. "He's coming back, and when he does, he's going to cut—" she shuddered as nausea swelled inside her "—cut off—" She couldn't say it. "I can't let them do that. What can you tell them that will satisfy them?"

Deke took her hand and put his lips to her ear. "Listen to me, Mindy. I swear I'd rather die myself than scare you, but you've got to understand what's going on here. There's *nothing* I can say that they'll be satisfied with. Nothing. Whatever I say, the end result is going to be the same."

Mindy's heart leapt into her throat. "End result?" she whispered brokenly. "What do you mean?"

He shook his head. "You know what I mean. Can you act like you're sleepy? We can't keep up this talking for their benefit. I've got something I need to do."

Mindy sat up straight and spoke aloud. "I guess all this is catching up to me. I'm so tired, and I'm feeing some minor contractions."

"Contractions?" Deke said. "You're not going into labor, are you?"

"The drug is still working, but I do need to rest. Do you think it's okay if I sit down in the chair and try to sleep a little?"

He nodded, then quirked his mouth. "Sure, hon," he drawled. "You've got about forty minutes to nap until they come back to cut off my finger."

Even though she knew he was talking for whoever was listening, the words still made her wince.

"Deke, I didn't—"

"Drag the chair over here," he said. "You won't be able to sleep sitting straight up in that chair. At least over here you can lean against me."

"That's very nice of you," she said stiffly. "I'll do that. And just so you know, I really don't want them to hurt you."

"Hmph. Good to know. Thanks."

She made a face at him and dragged the chair, slowly and loudly, over beside his desk chair, which was just opposite the door, and made a production of sitting down in it.

"Oh," she sighed. "I am so tired. You're sweet to let me lean on you."

Once she was settled in the chair, Deke whispered, "Did they bring you in here through that foyer?"

She nodded.

"So this room is the third door?"

"Yes, why?"

"I may have a way for us to escape."

Mindy's hand flew to her mouth. She couldn't help it. She'd tried hard not to think about their fate, but when she heard Deke's words, she realized that a large part of her had actually believed that they wouldn't live through this.

He put his hand on top of hers and shook his head. "Not foolproof. It's extremely dangerous. We could die."

And there it was. The one thing she'd counted on was Deke's strength and confidence. But if he thought they could die—

She felt the blood drain from her face, felt a hideous chill run down her spine. "Okay," she whispered.

"I'll do everything I can to make sure you're safe."

"*We're* safe."

He nodded, but he didn't look at her.

"So what do I need to do?"

"Go into labor."

A short, sharp laugh escaped her lips.

He held up a warning hand. "Mindy, you okay?" he said aloud.

"Oh," she responded. "What? I was asleep."

"You were dreaming. Go back to sleep."

"Go into labor?" she mouthed. Had she heard him right? He was whispering so softly she couldn't be sure.

He nodded. "I need a distraction so I can get the drop on them when they come into the room."

"Deke, you're injured and weak as a kitten. I doubt you could get the drop on a mouse."

His turn to make a face. "Well, I'm your only hope."

"Tell me what your plan is." She waited while he scrutinized her.

"I'm going to blow up the tunnel."

This time she clamped both hands over her mouth and stared at him over her fingers.

He put his hand over hers and held it there. "Dynamite," he mouthed.

She started to speak, but he shook his head. "Don't even ask. Just do what I say."

"But if you blow it up—" Her brain was filled with visions of smoke and rocks and dirt and body parts.

"And don't tell me you can't run. When I say run, you run. Your job is to save your—our—Sprout there."

Her hands flew to her tummy.

"They'll be in any minute." He scooped up the cut ropes they'd used to bind her hands. "Sit. Put your hands in your lap."

She did as he instructed, and within a few seconds he had the ropes arranged so she looked like she was still tied up.

Then he leaned back down and whispered in her ear. "There. That'll fool them on first glance. Once I take them down, we'll have about thirty seconds. Now, start faking labor."

She turned her head until her mouth was next to his ear. As much as she wanted to lay her cheek against his, just for a second, she knew she had to stay strong. "What are you going to do?"

"Hide behind the door."

"And do what? Slam it on them?"

Deke shook his head. "I've got the knife and a Taser. As soon as I take them down, you run out the south door into the foyer. I pried some boards off the trap door before they heard me and stopped me. Then get up the stairs and out. Remember what I said about my car?"

She nodded, feeling stunned. As far as she was concerned, he was telling her a fairy tale. There was no way she could climb through the trap door, run up the basement stairs and out to his car—not in her condition. But she'd try. She'd die trying, if that was her only chance.

As long as Deke didn't give up, she wasn't going to.

"Remember what I told you? If Irina's men aren't there yet, there's a cell phone under the driver's seat with the keys. Press Call for Irina's number, then turn the car around and drive away from the house as fast as you can."

"What about you?"

"I can take care of myself." Deke turned and placed himself behind the door, so that when it swung open, he'd be in the perfect position to get the drop on their attackers. He held the portable Taser in his weaker right hand and the knife in his left.

As she watched, he adjusted the dial on the Taser down and held it against his hand. He hit the switch. His fingers contracted.

He looked up with a small smile on his face. "It works."

She gave him a thumbs-up.

He twisted the dial up to maximum, then paused and sighed. He raised his gaze. "Mindy—" His whisper carried across the distance between them. "Don't—give up on me, okay?"

Her eyes filled with tears that spilled down her cheeks. "I never have. I never would," she whispered.

"Okay, ready?" he asked.

"Should I talk out loud?"

He shrugged. "Whatever you think will convince them."

Mindy started moaning, as if in her sleep.

Deke stood behind the door, balanced on the balls of his feet in attack mode. He watched Mindy in admiration. She scrunched her face up, as if in pain, and began blowing air out through her mouth. She was acting just like she had when she'd gone into premature labor down in the mine.

A chill slid down his spine. What if she really went into labor? He had no idea what a woman in labor could or couldn't do, but he was pretty sure climbing stairs and running was way down on the list.

She groaned louder and started pushing air through her mouth in little bursts.

Deke waited. He wished he knew what time it was, and how long it would be before James burst in. He normally had a good sense of time, but there were too many factors working against him here.

He was weak and shaky from blood loss and infection, and for the first time in his life he was questioning his own judgment. He had no idea whether he could hold his own against James and his soldiers.

And then there was Mindy. He looked over at her.

Her hair was tangled and stringy. Her eyes had deep shadows underneath them. The skin of her face was tight and drawn across her cheekbones. She was still the most beautiful thing he'd ever laid eyes on.

She was as brave as any soldier he'd fought alongside, but bravery alone didn't win battles. He knew she would push to the ends of her endurance to save the baby she cradled within her, but he was desperately afraid that wouldn't be enough. And he was terrified that he was asking too much of her.

He wasn't sure if he could survive if something happened to her or to his son.

His son. He had a son to fight for. A piece of him. His own flesh and blood.

He straightened his back and tightened his fists around the Taser and the knife. He had one chance to prove himself worthy of being a father. He would win, or he'd go down fighting for his wife and child.

"Deke? I'm getting worried. My contractions are getting stronger." She spoke aloud.

"Try to hang in there. Do you need to lie down?"

"I—may in a few—minutes," she gasped.

"Hey! James!" he shouted at the ceiling. "My wife's in labor. Help!"

He rocked up to the balls of his feet and readied himself. He knew James wouldn't come in here alone, and he fully expected that he and whoever came with him would be armed.

Glancing over at Mindy as she simulated the sounds and actions of a woman in labor, he saw his fear reflected in her eyes. He quirked his mouth in a smile, hoping to reassure her.

She wasn't fooled.

Then he heard footsteps outside the door. He caught her gaze and gestured toward the door with his head. "Here they are," he mouthed. He tensed, ready to spring—not on the first man. That would be suicide. He had to wait for the second, and hope there were only two.

The door slammed open and he flattened himself against the wall so it wouldn't hit him. Frank James walked in, followed by a soldier with a rifle cradled casually in his arms. The soldier had barely cleared the edge of the door by the time James realized that Deke wasn't in the desk chair.

"What's going on—?" he started.

The soldier reacted almost as fast. He raised the rifle.

As he did, Deke reached out and looped his left arm through the rifle's sling and jerked as hard as he could. He jabbed the Taser into the soldier's solar plexus and zapped him with a whopping dose of electric current.

The soldier shrieked and collapsed.

Deke jerked the rifle out of the soldier's limp hands and, in a single sweeping motion, swung it in an arc, slamming the butt into James's shoulder and knocking him aside.

He saw the flash of silver as James tumbled and immediately righted himself. He held a revolver.

"Get out, Mindy!" he yelled, as he lunged toward the gun. If James was still playing his game of Russian roulette, Deke might be able to overpower the fake cowboy before he could fire enough times to get to the live round. Or he might go down on the first pull of the trigger.

"Deke!" Mindy cried.

"Go, damn it."

He couldn't afford two seconds to turn his head and make sure she made it safely out the door. He got a good grip on the rifle and pushed the barrel into James's chest.

"I'll blow your heart right out of your chest, you sadistic bastard."

James's eyes widened in terror, but his shaky hand pulled the trigger on the revolver.

Even as Deke cringed, waiting for the hollow click of the hammer or the impact of the bullet, he bent down and Tasered James in the neck. As the hammer clicked impotently, James's body arched then went limp.

Deke grabbed the revolver.

He whirled and headed toward the door. As he stepped over the soldier, the man reached out and grabbed his boot.

He almost stumbled, but recovered himself and kicked backward, dislodging the soldier's hand.

Damn, with the dose of current he'd used, he'd have thought both of them would have been out of commission for several minutes at least.

The soldier tried to push himself up, but his arms collapsed. He screamed in a language Deke didn't understand, but the meaning was clear.

He was calling for help. Any second now, his buddies would burst in.

Deke had to get out of there.

He zapped the soldier again, but from the sound and the soldier's diminished reaction, he knew the Taser was almost out of juice. So he rammed the butt of the rifle into the man's head. At this point Deke didn't care whether any of them survived or not. They were terrorists.

Enemies of the United States. And they'd tried to hurt Mindy.

Still carrying both the revolver and the automatic rifle, Deke rushed through the door.

He didn't see Mindy anywhere. "Mindy!" he called.

Nothing. Dear God, he hoped she'd gotten out and up the stairs. "Min!" he yelled. "Run!"

He slammed the door into the foyer, wishing he had something to block it with. But there was no time for wishes.

He ran to the abandoned tunnel, carefully scooped up a double handful of blasting caps and slid them across the dirt floor to the foyer door. He ducked back into the tunnel as they clattered against the door. None of them went off from the impact.

Leaning back against the wall, he gulped in a huge breath, hoping it would clear his head. His arm burned, and he felt so sleepy. If he could just close his eyes for a couple of minutes…

No! Closing his eyes was giving up. Whatever strength he had left in him would go to making sure Mindy got to safety. He hadn't told her, but he was afraid Frank's men might have found his car, or that Irina might not have been able to zero in on his shoulder chip.

That car was her only chance. He needed her to trust that it was safe.

Digging in his pocket, he pulled out the disposable lighter and flicked it with his thumb. Spark but no flame.

Not now! He flicked it again, and again. *Light, damn it! I did not use all the butane!*

Finally a weak flame appeared. He paused. Had Mindy made it out of the building?

Please, God.

He waited a few more seconds—as long as he dared, before lighting the fuse, holding his breath with apprehension until it caught.

Then he rushed for the trapdoor.

Shouts and thundering footsteps filled his ears. He dove through the opening into the hotel's basement and right into the path of two soldiers careering down the stairs.

One of them grabbed him by the collar, and the other pointed a combat rifle at him and shouted something in a foreign language.

Deke raised his hands. The soldier holding his collar kicked him behind the knees and he fell to the ground.

"Dynamite!" he yelled. "Back there."

Whoever was in the foyer was banging on the door, trying to get through.

The soldier holding him yelled a warning at him and prodded his back with the rifle.

Deke didn't have to know the language to understand what the guy was saying

Shut up or die.

"Back there!" he shouted again. "Boom boom!" Wasn't *boom* the same in every language?

The sound of splintering wood told him that the soldiers had broken through the door to the foyer. He held his breath, and squeezed his eyes shut, trying not to think about what all those blasting caps would do when stepped on.

Sure enough, explosions like the sounds of giant firecrackers filled the air, followed by screams and shouts and the smell of gunpowder and burned metal.

In the next second, the hand on his collar let go, and both soldiers hit the ground.

Deke used their surprise and fear to push himself forward, toward the stairs. The dynamite was going to blow soon. He had to get out. If one of the soldiers recovered his wits and shot him, then so be it.

At least he'd die believing that Mindy had made it to safety.

He hit the stairs running, but with every step he climbed, his legs got heavier and slower.

A soldier yelled, and Deke instinctively flattened himself against the stairs. A bullet took a huge chunk out of the step near his head. He knew the man's next shot would be on target.

"Boom!" he yelled desperately. "Much more booms! Run!" Enveloped in a haze of drowsiness, he pulled together the last frayed threads of his strength and threw himself up the remaining steps.

A volley of bullets followed him. He stumbled through the door and spotted a patch of sunlight to his left. Was that the back door he'd told Mindy to look for? Or was just the flashing lights in his head signaling that he was about to pass out?

Didn't matter. Whatever the light was, it was his only hope for survival, because he heard heavy footsteps on the stairs behind him.

He staggered toward the light, noticing that it got brighter and dimmer at the same time. He shook his head, hoping he wasn't hallucinating, and grabbed at what looked like a door facing.

The light was bright and hot. And out in the distance, he saw two large uniformed men with a small figure in tow.

Mindy! They'd captured her.

He propelled himself forward just as a huge rumbling noise rose behind him and a blast of hot air slammed against his back, burning his skin.

It was over.

Tell Mindy I'm sorry.

Chapter Twelve

"Mindy, I'm sorry," Deke whispered brokenly through lips that wouldn't move. His mouth felt stuffed with cotton, and his head felt like it was made of lead. Helpless tears filled his eyes.

He hadn't wanted it to end like this. He would have gladly given his life for Mindy and their baby, but he had hoped he could have seen his son before he died.

"Mr. Cunningham?" A voice he didn't recognize was speaking very close to his ear. "Mr. Cunningham, are you awake? You need to wake up."

He wanted to swat at the annoying voice and sink back into oblivion, but he couldn't move his arm.

"We can't let you leave recovery until you wake up. Can you talk to me?"

Whoever was bothering him wasn't going to give up. He opened bleary eyes and then closed them immediately. The light was too bright. "Where's Mindy?"

"Mr. Cunningham, I need you to talk to *me.*"

"Leave me alone."

He heard a soft chuckle. "Well, that's something, I guess. Now open your eyes. Do you know where you are?"

Deke growled under his breath. If he couldn't see Mindy, he wanted to be left alone. He felt helpless—and feeling helpless pissed him off.

"In hell?" he muttered.

Another chuckle. "Not quite. You're in the recovery room, but now that I've got your attention, I'll make arrangements for you to be taken to your room. See this?"

He forced his eyes open and saw a blue plastic container that looked like it was made to hold a kidney. "I'm setting it right here beside you. If you feel sick, use it."

Whatever the woman was talking about, it didn't interest Deke in the least. All he cared about was finding Mindy. He sat up—or tried to. As soon as he raised his head, his vision went black.

Mindy! he screamed, but nobody answered.

DEKE OPENED HIS EYES. The last thing he remembered was the blast of exploding dynamite against his back.

No. There was something else he remembered—an annoying voice, but he couldn't place it.

He took a careful breath and was surprised at what he smelled. No heat, no burning cloth or wood—or flesh.

He smelled bleach, and something fresh and medicinal. He opened his eyes to a narrow slit. Everything was a muted green color.

Hospital! He was in a hospital. Suddenly he was wide-awake. That meant he hadn't been blown up when the dynamite exploded. And that meant—

Did that mean that Mindy was all right? And the baby?

He looked at himself. His left arm was bandaged

from elbow to wrist. There was a blood pressure cuff on his right upper arm and a needle sticking out of his wrist.

But not for long. He'd put in an IV port before, in the field. He could take one out.

And he did, with a little difficulty, hampered by the bandage on his right arm. The stick point bled a little, but he'd seen worse. Hell, he'd bled worse.

He slipped his arm out of the blood pressure cuff and sat up on the side of the bed—and discovered he had nothing on but the flimsy, open-backed hospital gown. He stood slowly, careful to give himself time to make sure his head was clear, then checked the closet and drawers. His clothes weren't there—not surprising. They'd been tattered and filthy. With a little digging, he found a set of scrubs—probably for him to wear when they discharged him.

He yanked off the gown and pulled on the scrub pants, stopping a time or two when his head began to spin.

By the time he got the pants on and the drawstring tied he was out of breath again. He took a long drink from a plastic water jug, letting a little of it drizzle down over his neck and chest. After rubbing it into his skin, he poured some in his hand and splashed his face.

Fortified by the water, he left his hospital room and headed down the hall to the nurse's station.

By the time he got there he was out of breath.

The ward clerk looked up from the orders she was transcribing. "Yes?" she said. "What room?"

"Where's my wife?" he demanded.

The clerk sighed. "What's your name and date of birth, please?"

"My room's right back there."

The clerk glanced past him. Deke turned and saw a security officer coming toward him.

"Take me to Mindy Cunningham," he demanded.

"Now Mr. Cunningham, I've been directed to see that you stay in your room. We need to make sure—"

"I need to make sure my *wife* is all right. Take me to her."

The guard held up his hands. "Now settle down—"

"No, you settle!" Deke's head was spinning again, but he took a step forward and got in the guard's face. "My wife was in labor. She'd better be here somewhere." He lowered his head and glared at the security guard from under his brows. "Take me to her—now!"

The guard nodded past him at the ward clerk.

The clerk typed a few keystrokes on a computer. "Room 410," she said.

"Where are the elevators?" Deke put a hand out to the wall to steady himself.

"Hold it. The only way you're going to leave this floor is in a wheelchair pushed by me. I have my orders."

"From who?"

The guard gestured at a nurse, who pushed a wheelchair up behind Deke. The guard put a hand on Deke's chest. Deke sank into the chair without a protest.

"From Irina Castle."

That shut Deke up for a few seconds. As the guard pushed him into the elevator, he finally found his voice. "Irina told you to make me use a wheelchair?" he asked suspiciously.

The security guard didn't answer him directly. He leaned forward and punched the button labeled 4. "She warned me that you'd be stubborn and difficult."

Deke watched the display as it showed 2, then 3 and finally 4. “Here we are.”

“Stay put. You don’t get to walk.”

As the guard pushed Deke out onto the fourth floor, he realized it was the maternity ward. The sight of yellow ducks and pink and blue elephants on the walls and the smell of baby powder rendered him speechless and paralyzed with fear.

Had Mindy had her baby? His baby?

Their baby?

The halls were filled with hospital employees dressed in pink and yellow and blue printed scrubs, carrying stacks of snowy-white linens, armfuls of tubing, pushing medication carts—he even saw one carrying an infant.

Then he saw the rooms and the numbers on the doors.

“Stop!”

The guard kept pushing the chair.

“Stop!” Deke put his bare foot out to try and stop the chair. He groped along the side until he found the lever that threw the brake.

“Hey!” the guard said.

“There’s room 410,” Deke snapped.

“Right. That’s where we’re headed.”

Deke turned his head and looked up at the guard from under his brows. “I’m not going in there in a wheelchair. She will *not* see me in a wheelchair, do you understand?”

He saw the guard’s Adam’s apple bob as he swallowed. “Yes.”

Deke stood. He had on nothing but green cotton pants and a bandage on his right arm, but at least he was standing on his own two feet.

It took him a couple of seconds to be sure he was steady enough to walk. The guard reached out a hand, but he shook his head.

A nurse walked up. "Are you Mr. Cunningham?" she asked.

He nodded. "Is my— Is Mindy—?"

The nurse smiled. "She just got back to her room."

"And the—"

"The baby is just fine. We'll be bringing him to her in a few minutes."

Deke's throat closed up.

The nurse patted his arm. "You can go on in."

He nodded.

The guard clasped him on the shoulder. "Congratulations, son."

Deke frowned at him for a second, then nodded. He waited until the nurse and the guard left before he stepped up to the closed door.

He put out his hand, but stopped short of pushing the door open. It wasn't fair to her to barge in on her without her permission.

Nothing had changed. Not really.

Mindy had never deserved what he'd put her through. His life was and always had been a train wreck, and she'd been dragged along with him for far too long.

She deserved to have the safe, normal life she'd always wanted.

He drew his hand back and wiped his face. One thing had changed. Him. At least now he could see how bad he was for her. What kind of danger she was in because of him.

Hell, if he had any courage at all, he'd turn and walk away.

THE OBSTETRICIAN HAD been very clear.

Relax! I want you to sleep at least twelve hours a day if not more. Every time your baby sleeps, you sleep.

Easy for you to say, she'd responded. She was too tired—and too tense to sleep. After three days of unrelenting fear and tension as she and Deke ran from terrorists, she'd barely had enough strength to assist in her Sprout's birth.

The doctor had threatened several times to do a Caesarian, but she'd refused every time.

"I'm fine," she'd puffed in the middle of her contractions. "I want to have him naturally. I want to see him the very instant he comes out, and I can*not* be confined to bed."

The doctor hadn't been happy, but Mindy had won. She'd told the doctor the truth, but not the whole truth. There was no way she'd let the doctor cut on her because as soon as she was able, she was going to find Deke.

In fact, she was just about to get up now. She took a deep breath that turned into a jaw-cracking yawn. She closed her eyes. After a couple of minutes of rest, she was definitely going to go searching for Deke.

The last glimpse she'd had of him was when he'd stumbled out the back door of the old hotel. In the very next instant, he'd disappeared in a cloud of black smoke as the building behind him had exploded.

She'd screamed and tried to run toward the burning building, but men in black secret service jackets had forced her into their SUV and rushed her with sirens wailing to Crook County Hospital's Maternity Ward. She'd screamed in protest until one of them made a call and verified for her that Deke was alive and on the way to the same hospital.

By the time Sprout had made his appearance, Mindy had made such a pest of herself that one of the labor and delivery nurses had checked with hospital admissions and found that he'd been admitted and rushed into surgery.

And that was all she'd been able to find out. Everyone seemed much more concerned with her resting and getting plenty of IV fluids.

She knew the nurses were going to be bringing little Sprout in to her within the hour, and her arms and heart ached to hold him. But she *knew* her baby was fine. She'd seen him briefly, and the doctor had reassured her that he had all the requisite fingers and toes.

She had no idea how Deke was. She had to find out if he was all right.

Dear God, please let him be all right. Let him be whole and well. And don't scar him any more than you have to, God.

Tears seeped out from underneath her closed lids. She knew scars wouldn't matter to him. She could hear him now. He'd say that the scars on the outside were a good match for the scars inside.

He'd endured so much. Been through so many trials, and kept his sanity and his goodness. If anybody in the world had earned the right to be happy, he had.

But his childhood had left such a mark on him. He was so afraid that he wasn't worthy of being a father. So afraid of being like his own father.

She wished she could convince him that he was nothing like Jim Cunningham. Deke's father had been a sick, lonely old man who'd wallowed in his own misery. He might have been a good man once, but he'd let drink and bitterness overwhelm him until he was consumed by self-hatred.

Deke had never let anything—not alcohol, not torture, not even heartbreak, overwhelm him. His innate goodness, combined with the love and trust of his friends, had kept him from veering onto the path his father had taken.

She just wished he believed in himself as much as everyone believed in him. Deke was a hero. He just didn't know it.

Mindy let her head recline back on the pillow, not caring that tears slid down her cheeks and neck. She'd never been able to break through the armor he'd built around his heart. Never been able to convince him of the kind of man he was. What made her think that she could now? It broke her heart that he might never accept that he deserved to be a part of his son's life or, more important, how much his son needed and deserved to have him as a father.

"You're a hero, Deke. Your son needs you, and so do I."

The door to her room eased open with a small squeak.

It was the nurse bringing her baby. Mindy smiled and pushed herself up in the bed.

"Come in," she called. "I've been wait—"

The hand that grasped the edge of the door was not a nurse's hand. It was big and long-fingered, with ragged nails, scraped knuckles and a specks of dried blood coating its back.

Mindy couldn't breathe as the door swung open and Deke stepped into the room.

He had on nothing but green scrub pants that hung low on his lean hips. His right arm was bandaged and the cut on his forehead was striped with sterile strips. His torso was an abstract painting in blues and purples and greens.

He looked exhausted and sick and scared. His blue eyes glittered in contrast to his pale face.

To Mindy, he'd always been larger than life. At over six feet, he towered over her five feet seven inches. But the physical difference between them had paled in comparison to his *presence.*

Now, however, standing half-naked in front of her, with all his hurts exposed, he seemed smaller, thinner. He looked human and breakable.

And she loved him so much that the mere sight of him stole her breath and hurt her heart.

She held out her hand. "Deke."

Deke stared at Mindy, unable to move. Hardly able to breathe. To his hazy brain, she looked like an angel, lying in the glow of the dim light that shone down from over the head of her bed. Her hair lay against the pale green sheets like dark angel wings.

He swallowed. "Can I—come in?" he said hoarsely.

She stared at him for a few seconds. Then her tongue flicked out to moisten her lips and his heart skipped a beat.

She nodded, still holding out her hand.

He stepped over to the side of the bed and took her hand in his. This close he could see the purple shadows under her eyes and the drawn translucence of her skin.

"Where's Sprout? I mean, have you—?"

She nodded. "They'll be bringing him in here in a few minutes."

A hot flash of pure panic ripped through him. "I should go."

Mindy's hand tightened on his. "Oh, no, you don't," she said. "You're not getting away that easily. Sit down here and tell me what happened."

He nodded. Sitting down would be a good idea right now. He gingerly perched on the edge of the bed, wincing as the movement made his bandaged arm ache.

"How's your arm?"

"I think it's going to be okay. I was supposed to wait for the doctor to come talk to me, but I needed to find you."

Mindy's eyes turned bright with tears. "That's funny. I was just about to go looking for you," she whispered. Her fingers slid back and forth across his knuckles. "The hotel blew up."

"Dynamite."

"What about James, and—?"

He shook his head, his lips flattened into a straight grim line. "I don't know."

Her hand squeezed his. "It had to be done, Deke."

"I know." He looked down at their hands. "Min, I'm glad you're okay. You and the baby." He paused, almost overwhelmed by all the emotions swirling through him. Love, fear, relief, sadness. "Really glad."

"I'm glad you're okay, too. I was so afraid—"

He nodded. "Do you remember how we got to the hospital?"

"Your car was surrounded by black SUVs when I got outside. I was terrified, but the men said they were Secret Service. I had no choice but to believe them. I got the feeling they would have gotten me into one of the vehicles one way or another."

"Secret Service. Aaron must have given them my

location. Or maybe Rafe tracked me by the chip." He rubbed his shoulder.

"Chip?" Mindy's eyes widened. "You told me—"

A sharp rap at the door made them both jump.

"Hi, Mindy," a cheerful voice said. "You've got a little visitor." The overhead light came on, chasing every last shadow from the room.

Deke's chest tightened. He had an overwhelming desire to bolt; to run as fast as he could somewhere—anywhere—as long as it was far away from the tiny baby that he was about to see.

He vaulted to his feet and backed away from the bed.

"Oh, hello." The nurse said. "You must be Mr. Cunningham. Congratulations."

All Deke could manage was a brief nod. He was too busy staring at the tiny baby the nurse was placing in Mindy's arms.

How could such a little thing cause so much of a stir? The whole room was alive with its presence. Mindy was glowing like a real angel. Her face was filled with a love and serenity he'd never seen before. He almost had to turn away from her beauty and happiness.

The nurse glanced from Deke to Mindy. She cleared her throat. "Well, why don't I come back in about a half hour? I can help you get started nursing him." She backed out of the room, turning off the glaring overhead light as she left.

Mindy smiled at her little Sprout. She'd held him for a few minutes in the delivery room, but there had been doctors and nurses all around, rattling instruments, cleaning and talking, and obviously impatient to clear the room and bring in the next delivery.

Now it was just him and her—and Deke. She touched

the little nose, the impossibly soft cheek. She held a finger for him to wrap his tiny fist around.

"Deke, look at his little fingernails." She kissed his fingers and rubbed her nose on his brand-new little arm. "He's so soft. So perfect."

She looked up at her ex-husband, and her heart twisted painfully in her chest. He'd been pale before, but now he looked positively ashen. If this were a sitcom, the audience would be laughing, she thought. But it wasn't a sitcom. This was real life, and Deke Cunningham had finally met his match.

"Come look at him," she coaxed, sending him a smile.

But he seemed to be frozen in place. His throat moved as he swallowed. His eyes looked huge and terrified.

Just moments before, Mindy had been worried about how he would react to their baby. But now that he was standing here in front of her, enveloped in paralyzing fear that not even the threat of death—not even the threat of *her* death—had raised in him, she was furious.

"Is this it, then?" she whispered fiercely, trying not to disturb the baby. "With everything that you've faced, the great, brave Deke Cunningham is going to be taken down by a six-pound newborn?"

She pressed her cheek against the top of her son's head for an instant, reassuring him.

Deke didn't move. He just stared at her.

"You're a coward. If you don't know by now what a wonderful father you'd make, then maybe you don't deserve him. Look at him. How could a bad person produce such a beautiful baby?"

"My father—" he started, but she cut him off.

"You know what? I know your dad hurt you, physically and emotionally. But my guess is he did the best he could. He just wasn't as strong as you. Maybe you got your strength from your mother. Or maybe something broke inside him." She took a shaky breath to try and calm her racing heart.

"I'm not excusing him, but maybe he couldn't handle life alone after your mother left. I don't know. What I do know is you are not your father. You are a hero, and the bravest man I've ever known. But if you can't face fatherhood, then I guess you're not as brave as I thought you were."

Had she gone too far? Too late now. She lifted her chin and met Deke's gaze. He either believed in himself or he didn't. the next few seconds might decide the rest of their lives.

He swallowed again and glanced down at the baby cradled in her arms, then looked back up to meet her gaze. "What—what do I do?"

"Come over here and sit down." Her scalp burned with relief, and her hands shook. But she wasn't about to show him how worried she'd been that he'd turn and bolt. She sat up a little straighter.

Deke looked like he was taking the last two steps to the gallows. But he finally sat down on the edge of the bed.

"Here," she said. "Take him in your left arm. Tuck his head right in the bend of your elbow."

Deke took the baby in the crook of his arm. His head was bowed and his hair covered his face. All she could tell was that he was looking at their son.

"He's little," he whispered.

"Thank goodness," Mindy said.

She heard him chuckle. Then he bent his head and pressed a kiss to his son's temple.

"You're almost as beautiful as your mother," he whispered. "I love you, Sprout."

Mindy's heart melted. He'd told his son he loved him, and the hitch in his voice let Mindy know that he'd never meant anything so much in his life.

He was going to be okay.

She watched him staring at his son. She could make it without Deke now. Now that she knew there was one person who'd broken through the wall around his heart. Knowing how much he loved their son was enough—almost.

LESS THAN TWELVE HOURS LATER, Deke sat in a borrowed conference room at the hospital, facing Mike Taylor, the new Secret Service agent in charge of the security detail assigned to Castle Ranch. He'd arrived just after Aimee Vick's baby was kidnapped.

He'd tried his damnedest to get discharged, but the nurses had told him he couldn't leave for another twenty-four hours.

In the chair next to Deke, looking as if she'd seen a ghost, sat Irina. On her left was Brock O'Neill. His carefully stiff demeanor, combined with the Bluetooth device in his ear, made him look more like a Secret Service agent than the casually dressed Taylor. On the other hand, the black patch over one eye made him look like a pirate.

But it was Taylor who had just dropped the bombshell. He'd just told Deke in his soft, careful voice that someone had tried to kill Irina.

"Tried?" Deke echoed. He reached out and touched

Irina's arm. "Are you okay?" he asked her while at the same time looking over her shoulder at Brock O'Neill.

She nodded, but he could feel the fine tremors that shook her body.

Brock's black gaze flickered. He had something to say, and he wanted to say it to Deke alone.

"What happened—and when?"

"I'm okay," she said quietly. "As soon as I heard that they'd found you and Mindy, I wanted to come and see you—"

"Thirty-five minutes ago," Taylor said. "Bastard was bold enough. It happened in the parking lot of the hospital."

Deke sat up, cradling his bandaged arm. "Here? I didn't hear anything."

"You wouldn't. Nobody did. It was a sniper, from who knows how far away. I've got men out searching for his nest, but—" Taylor shook his head.

Deke understood perfectly. He knew the range of the weapons he'd shot, and it was expansive. "Can you estimate the trajectory? The height? I can help—"

"Deke," Irina said, laying a hand on his left arm. "That's not all."

Her voice was tight. He met her gaze and saw tears.

"What? Who was shot?"

She shook her head. "Brock tried to talk me out of coming, but Rafe told me he'd come with me. So Brock told Rafe and Aaron both to bring me."

Deke met Brock's gaze again and knew he'd been right to trust the ex-navy SEAL. Brock knew what Deke knew. Either Aaron or Rafe was Novus's mole.

"What happened?" He directed that question at Mike.

"Rafiq Jackson was shot. The shooter got off three

rounds, then disappeared. Got Jackson in the meaty part of his thigh. Missed the artery. Damn lucky."

Damn good shot, Deke thought. "What about Aaron?" he asked.

"Narrow miss. The bullet grazed the skin right behind his temple. Both Gold and Jackson handled things well. The third round ricocheted off the top of Mrs. Castle's car. Your specialists both stated that a fifth of a second sooner and she'd have been hit between the eyes." Mike sent Irina a quick apologetic glance. "Sorry, Mrs. Castle."

She shook her head.

"Where's Rafe? And Aaron?"

"Jackson was rushed right up to surgery. Gold is in the emergency room. I'm about to go down there and debrief him."

Deke looked at Irina. "Would you like to go see Mindy and the baby for a few minutes?"

Irina's eyes darkened and she started to say something. But within a split second, she changed her mind and decided to do what Deke asked.

"I'll talk to you later," she said pointedly.

Deke nodded, suppressing a small smile. She was as gutsy as she'd always been.

He waited until she was out of the room.

"What the hell?" he asked Brock. "Which one?"

Taylor stayed quiet, but he was all ears.

Brock shook his head a fraction of an inch in each direction. "They're both spooked. Jackson was sure his femoral artery had been sliced. Gold knows he was about two millimeters from being toast."

"I know there are some sharpshooters out there, but you think those two shots were on target?"

Brock snorted.

Deke sent the Secret Service agent a sidelong glance.

"What?" Taylor demanded.

"This man could have nicked Jackson's femoral and given Gold a pierced ear," Brock said.

Taylor's mouth turned up slightly. "I heard you were good, Cunningham. I get the message. How do you want to handle it?"

"How many men can you put on my specialists while they're here at the hospital?" Deke asked.

Mike opened his mouth, but he waved his hand. "Figure it out, and figure out how many more you can place on the ranch. Novus is getting desperate and careless. He's failed twice—first Matt and now me. This sniper attack is showing us that he's willing to go to any lengths to get Irina." Deke paused. He didn't want to say anything more out loud. There was no telling who might be listening.

"Get Irina back to the ranch, and put every man you've got available on security. I'll be out to talk to you later today."

Taylor shifted uncomfortably. "I say we take Mrs. Castle to Washington, where we can ensure her safety."

Brock folded his arms across his chest.

Deke shook his head. "We'll lose Novus if we do that. She's got to be here."

"You're using her as *bait?*"

Deke couldn't explain the real reason he needed to keep Irina close. So he nodded. "Find where the sniper's nest was. As soon as I get out of here I want to see it. I might be able to tell you who it was."

He turned to Brock. "Will you wait here until Rafe's out of surgery?"

Brock nodded and left the room.

Taylor watched him until the door closed behind him, then he turned to Deke. "I'd sure like to know why you're able to command this much manpower from this high up in the government."

Deke didn't acknowledge his question. "Don't let Irina out of your sight, please. And I mean *your* sight, until she's safely back at the ranch. I'll be out of here this afternoon. I'll want to talk to you after dark."

Taylor gave Deke a brief nod and left the room.

Deke looked around the room. On a side table in the far corner of the large room was a telephone. For an instant, Deke considered using it. But it would be too dangerous.

He left the conference room and stepped over to a receptionist's desk. "Are there still pay phones anywhere around here?"

The young woman looked up and smiled. "Yes, sir," she said. "In the elevator lobby." She nodded toward her right.

The telephone kiosks were hardly private, but that was okay. All he was going to do was listen. He entered a memorized phone card number, then entered the number he wanted to call.

After six rings, he heard a click.

One message.

Deke's heart rate sped up. He entered a six-digit PIN. After a few more clicks, he heard the message.

He pushed his breath out in a huge whooshing sigh. Then he entered the code for Repeat and listened again.

Then pressed Delete and hung up.

For a second, he closed his eyes and leaned against the tiny metal frame around the phone. Then he wiped a hand down his face and punched the elevator call button.

Irina was coming out of Mindy's room when he got there. She had tears in her eyes.

"You are so blessed," she said, her voice a mixture of joy and tears. "Don't you dare mess this up."

He pulled back, not wanting to look her in the eye, but knowing she'd be suspicious if he didn't. "Yes, ma'am." He smiled.

But it didn't fool her for a second. Her brows drew down in a frown. "What's the matter? Is Rafe all right?"

"He's fine." Dear God, he wanted to tell her what he'd just found out. But he couldn't. No way. Even with everything that had happened, the worst still wasn't over.

In fact, the real battle hadn't even started, although it was about to.

Irina held his gaze for a beat, then nodded. "Good. Now get in there with your wife and son."

As Irina walked away, he rapped lightly on the open door, then stepped inside.

And stopped dead in his tracks.

Mindy was holding their son—nursing him.

"I'll— I can come back later," he stammered, awed and intimidated by the sight before him.

Mindy looked up and smiled. "Our little boy was very hungry."

He swallowed hard.

She laughed softly. "He's almost done. Want to hold him?"

Deke meant to shake his head no, but somehow it bobbed up and down instead.

"Come sit here."

He sat on the edge of the bed. "I don't know—"

"Don't worry. He's less fragile than he looks. I'm

going to put one hand under his head and one under his body. You take him the same way."

Deke did, amazed at how tiny and perfect he was. "Six pounds?" he whispered, staring at the tiny, scrunched-up face.

"And three ounces. He looks like you."

"How can you tell?"

"Oh, I can tell."

When Deke looked at her, his heart swelled so much he was sure it would burst out of his chest. "You are so beautiful."

"Liar." She touched her hair and smiled sheepishly.

"No," he said solemnly. "I've always thought you were the most beautiful thing I'd ever seen, although you may have a rival here." He nodded toward the precious baby he held. "But I don't think you've ever been as beautiful to me as you are right now. Min, I've broken too many promises. And God knows I don't deserve another chance, but—"

Mindy's eyes grew wide, but she didn't say anything.

"I want to *be* your husband. His father. Can we at least talk about it?"

For a long time she didn't say anything.

That's it then, he thought, bracing himself. He held Sprout closer to his chest.

"There's nothing to talk about," she whispered breathlessly.

Fear and dread certainty hit him like a blow. "There's not?"

She shook her head. "You *are* my husband. You *are* his father. You are my hero."

While Deke was still processing what she'd said, she

lay her palm against his stubbled cheek and raised her head to kiss him.

He kissed her back, holding their brand-new son between them.

* * * * *

The helicopter swung abruptly sideways in a dizzying arch, setting Jack McCall's fever-ravaged brain spinning.

His friend's voice sounded tinny, coming through the earphones. "You belong in a hospital," he said. "Not some backwater bed-and-breakfast."

All Jack really knew about the virus raging through his system was that it wasn't contagious, and there was no known treatment for it besides a lot of rest and quiet. "I don't like hospitals," he responded, hoping he sounded like his normal self. "They're full of sick people."

Vince Griffin chuckled but it was a dry sound, rough at the edges. "What's in Stone Creek, Arizona?" he asked. "Besides a whole lot of nothin'?"

Ashley O'Ballivan was in Stone Creek, and she was a whole lot of somethin', but Jack had neither the strength nor the inclination to explain. After the way he'd ducked out six months before, he didn't expect a welcome, knew he didn't deserve one. But Ashley, being Ashley, would take him in whatever her misgivings.

He had to get to Ashley; he'd be all right.

He closed his eyes, letting the fever swallow him.

There was no telling how much time had passed when he became aware of the chopper blades slowing overhead. Dimly, he saw the private ambulance waiting on the airfield outside of Stone Creek; it seemed that twilight had descended.

Jack sighed with relief. His clothes felt clammy against his flesh. His teeth began to chatter as two figures unloaded a gurney from the back of the ambulance and waited for the blades to stop.

"Great," Vince remarked, unsnapping his seat belt. "Those two look like volunteers, not real EMTs."

The chopper bounced sickeningly on its runners, and Vince, with a shake of his head, pushed open his door and jumped to the ground, head down.

Jack waited, wondering if he'd be able to stand on his own. After fumbling unsuccessfully with the buckle on his seat belt, he decided not.

When it was safe the EMTs approached, following Vince, who opened Jack's door.

His old friend Tanner Quinn stepped around Vince, his grin not quite reaching his eyes.

"You look like hell warmed over," he told Jack cheerfully.

"Since when are you an EMT?" Jack retorted.

Tanner reached in, wedged a shoulder under Jack's right arm and hauled him out of the chopper. His knees immediately buckled, and Vince stepped up, supporting him on the other side.

"In a place like Stone Creek," Tanner replied, "everybody helps out."

They reached the wheeled gurney, and Jack found himself on his back.

Tanner and the second man strapped him down, a process that brought back a few bad memories.

"Is there even a hospital in this place?" Vince asked irritably from somewhere in the night.

"There's a pretty good clinic over in Indian Rock," Tanner answered easily, "and it isn't far to Flagstaff." He paused to help his buddy hoist Jack and the gurney into the back of the ambulance. "You're in good hands, Jack. My wife is the best veterinarian in the state."

Jack laughed raggedly at that.

Vince muttered a curse.

Tanner climbed into the back beside him, perched on some kind of fold-down seat. The other man shut the doors.

"You in any pain?" Tanner said as his partner climbed into the driver's seat and started the engine.

"No." Jack looked up at his oldest and closest friend and wished he'd listened to Vince. Ever since he'd come down with the virus—a week after snatching a five-year-old girl back from her non-custodial parent, a small-time Colombian drug dealer—he hadn't been able to think about anyone or anything but Ashley. When he *could* think, anyway.

Now, in one of the first clearheaded moments he'd experienced since checking himself out of Bethesda the day before, he realized he might be making a major mistake. Not by facing Ashley—he owed her that much and a lot more. No, he could be putting her in danger, putting Tanner and his daughter and his pregnant wife in danger, too.

"I shouldn't have come here," he said, keeping his voice low.

Tanner shook his head, his jaw clamped down hard as though he was irritated by Jack's statement.

"This is where you belong," Tanner insisted. "If you'd had sense enough to know that six months ago, old buddy, when you bailed on Ashley without so much as a fare-thee-well, you wouldn't be in this mess."

Ashley. The name had run through his mind a million times in those six months, but hearing somebody say it out loud was like having a fist close around his insides and squeeze hard.

Jack couldn't speak.

Tanner didn't press for further conversation.

The ambulance bumped over country roads, finally hitting smooth blacktop.

"Here we are," Tanner said. "Ashley's place."

* * * * *

Will Jack be able to
patch things up with Ashley,
or will his past put the woman he loves
in harm's way?
Find out in
AT HOME IN STONE CREEK
by Linda Lael Miller
Available November 2009
from Silhouette Special Edition®

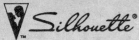

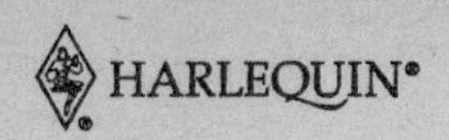

INTRIGUE®

COMING NEXT MONTH

Available November 10, 2009

#1167 BRAVO, TANGO, COWBOY by Joanna Wayne
Special Ops Texas
The svelte dancer caught the cowboy's eye on the dance floor, but as the former navy SEAL joins in the search for her kidnapped daughter, she may just steal his heart, as well.

#1168 THE COLONEL'S WIDOW? by Mallory Kane
Black Hills Brotherhood
Two years ago he made the ultimate sacrifice…he faked his own death to protect his wife from the terrorist he hunted. But now she is being targeted again, and the former air force officer will need to return from the dead to protect the woman he loves.

#1169 MAGNUM FORCE MAN by Amanda Stevens
Maximum Men
In all his years training at the Facility, there was only one woman who could draw him away—and she's in danger. Now he'll put all his abilities to work to save her.

#1170 TRUSTING A STRANGER by Kerry Connor
The only way to save her life and escape her ex-husband's enemies was to marry the attractive yet coldhearted American attorney. Neither expected their feelings would grow or that danger would follow her to her new home….

#1171 BODYGUARD UNDER THE MISTLETOE by Cassie Miles
Christmas at the Carlisles
Kidnappers used her ranch as a base of operations, and now she and her little girl are their target. But first they'll have to get past her self-appointed bodyguard—a man who won't rest until she's safe…and in his arms.

#1172 OPERATION XOXO by Elle James
Just when she thought she had outrun her past, the first threatening note arrived—then there was a murder. The FBI agent sent to protect her is as charming as he is lethal, but can she trust him enough to let down her own guard?